Praise for Soulmates

"Haunting, relentless, and sadomasochist in nature, *SOULMATES* by Jeremy Megargee offers readers pain and pleasure in equal measure. A truly terrifying and obsessive experience."—Grace R. Reynolds, Elgin Award-nominated author of *The Lies We Weave*

"Tormented and twisted, *Soulmates* will plant a flower in the rotted soil of your soul and show you love can blossom in the darkest of places." —Mona Kabbani, author of *The Bell Chime* & *Vanilla*

"A Clockwork Orange romance. Delicate, flowing prose set against characters' anguish and Megargee's signature carnage. What makes *Soulmates* a true gem is its dissection and reconstruction of souls we can't bear to look at yet can't help but love."—Spencer Hamilton, author *of I Will Devour You* and *Other Promises*

Soulmates

By Jeremy Megargee

Curious Corvid
PUBLISHING

Content Warnings

This work contains references to abuse, self-harm, sexual trauma, and violence.

Ambrose

Ambrose lies in the casket of self, and he hates how his dead flesh feels slack on the bones. His room is a pit of blackness, a cave for a lethargic bear that prefers hibernation with no end. He spends so much time in here that the hours bleed together until time ceases to hold any level of significance. He is a living corpse, so why try? It's shameful puppetry to drag his putrefied form out of the bed in an effort to succeed at civilization.

The only relationship Ambrose strives for is with entropy, and to wish for more is a fool's errand. He is expired meat, and it is best to hide from existence in this unplugged refrigerator until what remains of him returns to the weeds. When he looks in the mirror, he sees sludge and rot, a sack of organs that droops down into oblivion, and the bleary-eyed rage that fills him up threatens to leap out from the reflection. This isn't a life.

It's what is supposed to happen after a life reaches its inevitable conclusion.

The psychiatrists have all tried to reach him, but nothing passes through the fetid stew of his thoughts. He was diagnosed with Cotard's delusion, otherwise known as walking corpse syndrome. He's been prodded and examined by head doctors from all around the country, men and women with substantial academic pedigrees, but no matter what mental institution Ambrose vacations at, the final answer is always the same. He is alive on a biological level, but in his heart and his mind, he knows he is dead.

Ambrose can smell the rot that emanates from his pores. He can feel the rigor mortis that settles into his limbs when he rests. He can hear the maggots that squiggle and breed in the murky soup where his intestines should be. There is no convincing him that he's alive, and when the medical professionals try, Ambrose turns from them and stares at a wall until they lose interest.

Apathy is his security blanket, and he refuses to give it up. He bed rots for years at a time with no understanding of ambition, no goals to achieve, and nothing at all to make him feel like he has a place in this world. There are the glowing web strands of the internet, that place where he can pretend to be what he's not, and in those rare moments when he does leave his room, nothing he encounters outside of his four familiar walls seems real.

When you feel dead, you neglect yourself. You stop caring. A carcass isn't meant to care.

Dandelion

Whenever she dreams, she's always deep under the ocean, so far beyond the shallows and the seaweed. Her smooth young body sinks down by inches, passing through schools of tropical fish, her thighs scraping against the unrelenting edges of coral reefs. Dandelion chokes on salt, and the deeper she goes, the more she misses sunlight. Did it ever truly warm her skin, or were those sunbeams the real dream?

She feels like a lost thing that will never be recovered. A ballet shoe from the Titanic. The femur of a man who dared to sail around the globe. Some vague, forgotten object that drifts and pirouettes with the tide. There's no control down here, and on some level, Dandelion likes that. She thrives when she's in the passenger seat, for it is safer to let others drive. Easier to navigate the roadways of life when you're not responsible for what comes next.

But she doesn't like what waits down in those endless crevices—big, dark open mouths in the form of trenches that extend for miles. Canyons beneath the surface. And as she freefalls, arms languidly spinning, the fear that thrums in her heart awakens.

Deep-sea gigantism. Sometimes she can't stop thinking about it. She has fallen down more search engine rabbit holes than she can count, looking up pictures and videos of gargantuan creatures that live in the most remote underwater places that Earth has to offer.

She can feel that they're waiting down there for her. Enormous squid tentacles seeking to suckle and tease, looming hollow-toothed gorgons that make their own haunting turquoise light, and those creeping, giant sea spiders that skitter along in slow motion, seeking nutrition and the desecration of Dandelion petals.

She's screaming down there, the bubbles pulsing up all around her, and claws and fangs and jellied appendages reach up to comfort her, tracing out love letters on bare patches of thigh and abdomen. A banana-colored eel is slithering up, silver dollars for eyes, and as it comes closer, her legs open involuntarily, offering up easy access. Dandelion feels it nuzzle in, and she trembles at the act of violation.

It's a hard fight to wake up. Her hair is matted to her brow, and slobber drips down her chin to pool between her pierced nipples. Dandelion wipes it away and flings it from her, wanting to be free from even the idea of moisture.

She's in a nauseous sweat, and even in the raindrops that slide across her bedroom window, ghosts of undersea giants peer inward.

Ambrose

Ambrose walks in the night when everything is dim and silent, with only the low hum of streetlamps reverberating through the dripping meat blanket he calls a body. He feels bloodless, a bad cut left out on a butcher's block, and his destiny is the refuse bin.

His hood is tight against the wind, and it renders him virtually anonymous. Ambrose likes this just fine. He hates how he can feel the sinew and organ morsels slopping together inside of him, creating a brine in the sternum, and if he were to be stabbed tonight, he'd leak out ichor from a thousand shameful wounds.

Ambrose slides his eyes across the stars overheard, the few brave pinprick souls shining down through the industrial smog of the city. He fetches a sigh that dies in the night and dies in him. There should be meaning up there, a curiosity about the cosmos, but Ambrose's heart remains an empty drum. It's like his nerves are numb, his imagination zombified, and nothing stirs the deadness in the center of his brain.

He is fully sentient, possessed of his own will, personality intact, and he remembers a line from an old eighties zombie film that has always stuck with him:

"It hurts to be dead."

Oh, yes. More than anything.

Dandelion

There are some nights where the boredom and loneliness force a physical ache to awaken inside of Dandelion. It feels like hooked fangs chewing into her most sensitive parts and rag-dolling what is left of her across the seafloor. In these moments of weakness, she seeks the comfort of strangers. Omegle is her preferred medium when it comes to searching for meaning in the void. She turns on her webcam and flips through fellow lost souls on the internet, all of them seeking some manner of connection.

There's a lot of ugliness on Omegle, but it fascinates her. Old men cranking at their ruined elephant-trunk cocks. Masked fetishists that bark like a dog and smear excrement on themselves. Sad, young faces in dark rooms, voices yearning, and the longer she spends clicking through the webcam feed, the more she starts to feel like the entire universe is one vast

darkroom.

It's been the standard fare tonight. A few horny middle-aged men that she quickly skipped, and some dead accounts with nothing but static buzzing from smeared cameras. Dandelion's ocean-blue eyes reflect the glow of the laptop screen, and after about an hour of browsing, she lands on a person that catches her attention.

His appearance is mostly unremarkable. A dark hoodie nestled around his face, a few tufts of straw-colored hair peeking out to curl across his brow. His face is round, almost cherubic, but his eyes do something to her. They're the color of spilled oil, glimmering black holes in the form of irises, and when she makes direct eye contact with the young man, she feels a profound absence. There's this gnawing nothingness that comes out of him, leaking from the screen, and his facial expression is so slack and flat that she momentarily mistakes him for a cadaver that has been propped in front of a webcam.

She lifts up a hand in a little wave, mostly just to see if he reacts at all.

"Hi."

He slowly comes to life, a rusted robot left behind after some vague apocalypse. It's like he has to remember how to properly use his vocal cords.

"Hey."

"What's your name?"

"Ambrose. And yours?"

"I'm Dandelion."

His voice is a dried out whisper, and Dandelion has to lean close to her laptop's speakers in order to even hear him at all.

"Like the flower. Makes sense. Do you need sunlight to grow too?"

She chuckles despite herself.

"I don't get nearly enough of it. Kind of a homebody."

"It's safer indoors. The world is less loud when you're surrounded by walls that you can control."

Dandelion's face is practically up against the screen, eager to hear and equally eager to see. There's a fog in the background behind Ambrose, and it makes him look like he's sitting in the middle of Silent Hill. It takes her a minute to realize that it must be a cigarette smoldering in an ashtray somewhere off screen.

"You're a strange one, stranger."

"We don't have to be strangers. Wanna talk on this messenger app? Sometimes it's easier for me to write out what I'm thinking."

Ambrose sends a download link, and Dandelion usually wouldn't trust such a gesture. She worries about viruses and hackers digging into all the personal info she has on her computer, but this man has his hooks in her, and she cannot say why. Her curiosity is burning, and she wants to know more.

"Sure."

> Chat...

WatchMeRot: How do you feel about endings?

PetalsofDandelion: They can be hard. But why bring up endings? You and I talking now, it feels like a beginning.

WatchMeRot: It won't last. When it comes to people, nothing ever does.

PetalsofDandelion: You talk like you're not a person.

WatchMeRot: Most days I don't feel like one.

PetalsofDandelion: Why?

WatchMeRot: I have a condition. A mental disorder, but to me, it feels real. I feel dead. I feel like a corpse that was cursed with the burden to live and breathe. It distorts everything in my life.

PetalsofDandelion: But we're chatting now, so you can't be dead. You exist. You're using your living fingers to text me.

WatchMeRot: I've been told a thousand times that I am alive and it's all in my head. It doesn't help. It doesn't cure the decay, and the rot remains.

PetalsofDandelion: What's it like? To go through everyday life thinking you're already dead?

WatchMeRot: Problems matter less. The world seems wounded and washed out. I'm just a thing that should be in a pine box. It's harder to care. Harder just to *be*.

PetalsofDandelion: You're not alone. I have bad thoughts too.

WatchMeRot: Tell me.

PetalsofDandelion: I dream. Sometimes it feels like I never stop dreaming. I dream of water. I dream of depths. I dream of things that grow fat and swollen in black pressurized places. Enormous bodies, enormous appetites.

WatchMeRot: We all have appetites, Dandelion.

PetalsofDandelion: Yeah?

WatchMeRot: Even the dead dream.

PetalsofDandelion: Share with me? <3

WatchMeRot: Oh, where to start. . .

19

Chat...

PetalsofDandelion: I worry that I play it safe sometimes. I don't often take chances. I live in a safe little box and I almost never go beyond my comfort zone.

WatchMeRot: Are you afraid?

PetalsofDandelion: Yeah.

PetalsofDandelion: Help me.

WatchMeRot: We can start small. The only way to conquer a fear is to face it head on. Most of your nightmares involve water, right?

PetalsofDandelion: Not so much water, but what can lurk beneath the surface. Even rain makes me nervous, and the forecast is calling for it soon.

WatchMeRot: I want you to find a puddle after the morning rainstorm. Change into a bathing suit and sit in that puddle.

Stay there until the anxiety inside of you goes numb. And take

selfies while you're sitting in there and send them to me.

PetalsofDandelion: Why the pictures?

WatchMeRot: You need someone to hold you accountable. To

help you tighten fingers on the throat of fear and press firmly. I

can do that.

PetalsofDandelion: I'm self-conscious. I don't love my body.

There are some self-harm scars. Will that disgust you?

WatchMeRot: I give no thought to shallow cuts and shallow

waters. Together we go deep, Dandelion. Always deeper.

Promise?

PetalsofDandelion: Promise.

WatchMeRot: There might be things in the puddle. Larvae.

Tadpoles. Water bugs. They'll tickle, but no lasting harm will

come.

PetalsofDandelion: I trust you, Ambrose.

***

PetalsofDandelion: Did you get the pics? Do I look pretty?

WatchMeRot: You looked sad. Lost. Bruised, but not just the skin. Bruised down deep in the soul. I think you're haunted, Dandelion. There are so many ghosts in your eyes.

PetalsofDandelion: I'm sorry. I can do better next time.

WatchMeRot: You misunderstand. I liked the pictures. Your toes curling in the mud just out of frame, and the mosquitoes flying around your rainbow hair. What inspired you to dye your hair so many different colors at once?

PetalsofDandelion: Sometimes all the color drains out of the world for me. I feel intensely. The hair lets me capture some of that color when things get dark. I'm able to keep it.

WatchMeRot: What did you feel as you sat there? Be honest.

PetalsofDandelion: I felt like I wanted you to like me. I felt like my thoughts were tied to a balloon string and drifting far above. Nothing bad happened. A part of me thought a fissure would open in the earth and something huge would slither up from an underground river and eat me alive. But that didn't happen. I just sat there, splashing like a little kid, and I let the sun burn down and kiss my skin.

WatchMeRot: You were disciplined. That is one of my favorite qualities in a person.

PetalsofDandelion: I stayed sitting there for hours, just like you told me.

WatchMeRot: Good girl. Soon, when I know you're ready, we'll try other things.

Dandelion

Dandelion stands nude in front of the mirror in her room. It is crisscrossed with spider-web cracks and haphazardly mended with strips of black electrical tape. She has smashed it more times than she can count due to past emotional meltdowns, but each time that happens, she crawls around the dirty carpet and picks up the shards, usually crying softly to herself as she attempts to put it back together again.

She's trying not to cry now. She's examining her body the way a mortician would examine a corpse on the slab. Her gaze is clinical and passionless, and each scar, pimple, and stretch mark takes up a place of dominance in her head. She doesn't see the overall beauty even though many people in her life have told her that it exists. She sees only a jigsaw puzzle of flaws, and so many of her pieces have been dropped and discarded that she fears she might never be complete again.

There's a box cutter under her mattress, and that rusted blade is a siren song. It has split all the best parts of her open over and over again. Dandelion is craving it now, the sight of wounds like red mouths that gape wider each time she breathes. But she holds back. Restraint has never been her strong suit, so it surprises her.

It's because of Ambrose. She's been concocting fantasies in her head about the two of them meeting and creating some kind of a life together. She wants to be a good, presentable girl for him. He can't ever be permitted to see her as she truly is. A ruined doll covered in makeup and hair dye and tattoos, all of it a shield, a disguise to outweigh the ugliness that crawls through her insides.

The real her has to be buried down in the deepest pit of self. She will molt and evolve and shed snakeskin until she is exactly what she thinks he wants. No longer the blank mannequin, but a dream girl for him to fawn over.

She stares at her own body for a long time, hands running unkindly over skin, pinching and scratching and trying to endure the sight of herself.

What do dead boys truly desire?

Soulmates

┌──────────────────┐ Chat... └──────────────────┘

PetalsofDandelion: Ever been in love?

WatchMeRot: I don't think so.

PetalsofDandelion: Usually with something like love, you'd know for sure.

WatchMeRot: I struggle with feelings. Most days, it's hard to feel anything at all.

PetalsofDandelion: What do you imagine that being in love feels like?

WatchMeRot: A syringe of heated embalming fluid pumped into the veins. A cloud of gnats flying around inside of you and nibbling on your heart. Love has to be uncomfortable. Stressful. It should terrify, because there's risk involved.

PetalsofDandelion: I've loved many and often. Usually I love what doesn't love me back most of all.

WatchMeRot: There's a streak of self-destruction in you, Dandelion.

PetalsofDandelion: Oh darling, you have no idea. It's more than just a streak.

WatchMeRot: I like the idea of lovers being buried together. Bones clinging to bones. That's truth. That's eternity, and it can't be faked.

PetalsofDandelion: It's a beautiful concept.

PetalsofDandelion: Does Cotard's delusion have physical effects too? Like if I were to run my fingertips over your skin, would it be cold and clammy to the touch?

WatchMeRot: I think your fingers would sink in. It would be like caressing mushy rotten fruit. I'm sure to you, it would feel like you're touching a normal warm body. But to me, it would be like someone taking pity on a soulless touch-starved husk. I experience things differently.

PetalsofDandelion: I think that's part of your charm. And I think you're wrong.

WatchMeRot: About what?

PetalsofDandelion: I think beneath the false shroud of death, you do have a soul.

Ambrose

Rain hits differently when the whole world dies. Autumn itself is a time of ending. Ambrose thinks of endings as he crunches on dead leaves, listening to the brittle fracturing of golds and reds under boot heel. He thinks that his entire life has been an ending. No enthusiasm in his reflection, just a gray mottled face and eyes bled of hope.

But there is a change. In his dark ribcage where flayed meat hangs in a tattered curtain, a spark of some kind has started to flicker. It's not much. It's just a firefly that hasn't yet learned how to control its light, but to Ambrose, that means everything.

She's growing out of the rotten ground inside his brain. Just a single dandelion with petals that yearn for the sun. When he sees her screen name pop up on his phone, his mouth twitches involuntarily. It wants to smile. To stretch out the stiffened skin and make a real attempt at a warm expression.

He lifts up his palms and catches the rain, the canopies of the trees above him casting out long shadows on his cadaverous cheeks. There should be sensation, but there is not. If his cells were alive and functioning, he'd feel nourished by the rain. Awakened. But that isn't the case. There is just the ever-present numbness.

Will it be the same with her?

Lacking the ability to feel, connect, or savor existence. He can't let her go. She woke the firefly, and now its wings beat against his desiccated organs. Ambrose doesn't want an end, for once. He wants to keep Dandelion in a little jar on the windowsill. A terrarium of a girl to be watered and pruned and drowned in sweet soil.

Through him, she will grow.

Chat...

PetalsofDandelion: I can prove to you that you're alive.

WatchMeRot: I don't think that's possible.

PetalsofDandelion: Do you trust me?

WatchMeRot: I do.

PetalsofDandelion: It might seem a little extreme, but I think sometimes in life, extremes are called for. The human spirit is most potent in the presence of pain.

WatchMeRot: What kind of pain, Dandelion?

PetalsofDandelion: You have to remove one of your fingernails. Not a big one or an important one. It should be the pinky, because that's practically a useless finger, and no one would even notice if the nail is gone. But if you rip it out, it'll wake up the person deep within. The soul that is buried under all of those mounds of dead flesh.

WatchMeRot: I don't know. Physical pain doesn't have much of an impact on me. The mental pain seems to override it. If a corpse mutilates itself, there's no great pageantry in the act. It is still just a corpse after, but with new wounds for the vermin to explore.

PetalsofDandelion: Try it for me. You can use pliers, or maybe you can pull it back with the claw end of a hammer. Shatter it into splinters and pluck out the pieces. When you see that raw red nail bed, it might make you feel. I want you to feel, Ambrose. There is nothing worse than the dull absence of feeling, and I don't want that to be your forever.

WatchMeRot: We're certainly in agreement on that.

PetalsofDandelion: Tear out the fingernail, put it into an envelope, and mail it to me. I'll give you my address. It'll be a little part of you that I can keep close to me, and it'll make what is developing between us feel more real.

WatchMeRot: What will you do with it?

PetalsofDandelion: I'll dress it in pink silk, I'll find a tiny box for it, and it'll sleep with me in a little coffin all its own. When the night terrors come and the monsters from the deep bellow for me, I'll hold it tight. You'll protect me. Even from afar, you'll protect me.

WatchMeRot: I won't let them eat you up.

WatchMeRot: Let me find a good pair of pliers.

Ambrose

Blood in what seems like tidal waves. Exposed pink tissue that is never meant to see the light. The slow crack of pliers working against fingernail, yanking it from the root. The anguish should be considerable, but not for Ambrose.

It has always been this way with Cotard's delusion. His pain is a dim thing, a bulb lacking the will for incandescence. His body is stiff and poisoned with death, so a silly little sensation like pain has never really made much difference either way. His gaze is flat, listless, eyes staring into a grayscale dimension that only he can see. This isn't personal mutilation for Ambrose. It is just a chore that needs doing.

But he wants to feel something. He wants to feel for *her*. His body sways like a willow, and deep in the pit of hopeless decay, a songbird takes flight. It's a brief flash, a true taste of agony's potential, but it is enough to startle him. It comes when the nail frees itself fully, excised from the body, apart from the whole

now, and he holds it up to his eyes like a tiny ruined keepsake.

Ambrose searches for an envelope, leaving smeared crimson

handprints all over the kitchen counter. He nestles the nail in

gently, and he signs a brief note with the bleeding stub of his

pinky.

"You're right. I felt something."

—A.

Dandelion

She turns the fingernail over in her hands, marveling at it. It's just a tiny souvenir speckled in blood, but it carries great emotional weight in the center of her palm. Dandelion brings it up to her nose and sniffs, and the scent of a thousand graveyards assaults her. The aroma is pleasant to her, like a musk, cologne rising up from a dead man's skin.

She fashioned a matchbox into a miniature casket, soft silk within, but something overrides the urge to slide the fingernail into its new home. There's a compulsion slithering around inside of her. On certain dark, moonless nights when there is no one there to see, Dandelion rips tufts from her hair and eats them. She doesn't know why. She dare not tell a soul that she does it. It's never a significant amount of hair, and she's able to compensate by styling it differently. Through this strange obsession, she came to understand her own appetite.

Hunger lives in her, born of dark regions, and it wants what it wants. Saliva jets into her mouth, and she stands there frozen in the midday sun that burns through the windowpane. There is drool glistening on her chin, and, thankfully, no one around to judge her for it.

Dandelion lifts up the fingernail and carefully places it on her tongue, almost like she's taking a tab of ecstasy, and then she throws back her head and swallows.

It's scratchy as it travels down her throat, and when it is finally lodged deep inside, a bloom of contentment overtakes her body. She places both hands across her bare abdomen and looks down proudly, resembling a mother—to-be the first week after a positive pregnancy test.

A small piece of Ambrose lives in her now. Just a brittle crumb of death, but on some level, it helps her to feel what he feels.

Chat...

WatchMeRot: Did you like the fingernail?

PetalsofDandelion: I loved it. I have it in a special place.

WatchMeRot: I'm glad.

WatchMeRot: I've been having thoughts.

PetalsofDandelion: Oh?

WatchMeRot: I'm worried they might scare you away. They're nasty thoughts. Nasty ideas. I feel them slithering.

PetalsofDandelion: Let me be the judge of that. You'd be surprised at how willing I am to embrace the taboo.

WatchMeRot: My brain has felt like a pressure cooker. It's full of fantasies involving you. Stripped you, bruised you, yearning you. A version of you that is an exhibitionist.

PetalsofDandelion: Would that please you? Seeing me bare and reveling?

WatchMeRot: Not just that. I picture you in a rotting house. Splayed out and feral on mildewed floorboards, ass cheeks resting among rat nests and millipedes. A ruined wretched rotting place, but you love to be there, and you fall into a nameless ecstasy. You fuck yourself on that filthy floor. You leak out Dandelion juice and it drips down into a feculent basement that never sees the sun.

PetalsofDandelion: You want me to be dirty for you. A scummy little baby with cobwebs kissing at her cunt. That's what you like?

WatchMeRot: It's what I crave. I've never dabbled in drugs. I feel like they'd just turn to dust in my veins. But that image? You masturbating in an abandoned house and embracing the decay? I think it would be heroin for me.

PetalsofDandelion: I'll make an addict of you.

WatchMeRot: In many ways, you already have.

PetalsofDandelion: I know a place. It's little more than the skeleton of a house. Open to the elements and the wildlife.

PetalsofDandelion: I'll go there soon, and I'll be wild for you too.

Dandelion

It could have been a palace in a previous incarnation, but now the house is just splintered nothingness. It gapes with broken drywall teeth, and it invites the wind, and with the wind blows in a Dandelion. She drags fingertips over the remnants of flowered wallpaper, and there is the subtle sound of flattening spider eggs in the wake of her touch. There's a heavy aroma in here, and it hits her hard. It is carrion and neglect, the perfume of an unloved structure with sagging windows that cry whenever it rains.

Dandelion slinks deeper into empty rooms with warped floors and cinder-blackened ceilings. She moves forward and sets up her phone, leaning it against the tarnished brickwork of a fireplace. A single press of her thumb, and the little red eyes open to indicate that video is being recorded.

Her rainbow hair hangs down, wet from a shower, in her face, and her eyes are twinkles of quartz in the gloom. Moonlight spills over her, lighting on scarred, razor-kissed forearms and porcelain skin. She wears nothing because Ambrose requested that she wear nothing. Bare in this room of rot, the gooseflesh decorating each inch of her skin. This feels feral. It feels deranged.

Dandelion loves it.

She crumbles down to the floor, a boneless puppet, and she makes a show of opening her thighs wide for the camera. She beckons to a dead thing, fingers crawling over her most sensitive parts, and she draws forth a dollop of her own nectar and smears it across her tongue, lapping it up, with a hellgrin plastered ear to ear across her face.

She fucks herself and she tastes herself, and the subtle vibration of her movements causes dust to drift down from the ceiling, specks of it becoming lost in her soaked hair. Bats flap unsettled in the attic, and a coyote mother that has denned in the root cellar begins to yelp and howl at this human intrusion. The animals of the death house want her expelled, but she belongs here, and she will not rest until Ambrose has his treat.

Her moans echo off walls, and she moves toward the camera, wanting infinitely uncomfortable closeness. If it were viable, she'd pull the camera deep within and let him see all the colors of her insides.

When she cums, a portion of the house collapses around her. Dandelion remains completely unharmed in a circle of rubble. She luxuriates in herself, pinwheeling naked arms and legs, embracing her own shape, the form of Venus on a filthy fuckdoll floor.

After her orgasm, she begins to scream for no comprehensible reason at all. It is guttural and tormented and lost, and it goes on for what seems an age. The camera captures it all, even the moment when Dandelion crawls over to retrieve it.

She hopes very much that Ambrose will be proud of her performance.

Ambrose

He watches the video on repeat over and over again until his eyeballs feel dry in their sockets. She's like a succubus making a playground of degradation, and Ambrose cannot peel his gaze away from her facial expressions. He imagines that Dandelion tastes like blueberries and mangos, but just a little spoiled, a little rotten, and he longs to devour the fruiting mush that lingers in her body. There's so much emotion in her eyes as she touches herself for him, and he thinks that she looks like a fallen fairy, wings torn out for some unspeakable act she committed that can never be forgiven.

Usually his libido feels as dead as the rest of him, but not for her. There's a subtle change to his physiology. His neglected cock wakes from a hibernation of decades, and it rises like a swaying cobra in his jeans, threatening to spurt poison even without him having to place a single finger along the length of the shaft. This is the impact that she has on him. It is ungodly, and he never wants it to end.

Ambrose would make himself mincemeat for her if she asked. He'd throw himself into an industrial meat grinder and encourage her to lap up the dead fleshy bits from the floor. Due to his battle with Cotard's delusion, he's never been able to form a healthy concept of sexual attraction or how to expel his desires. It is all tainted and twisted in his head, but he doesn't think that Dandelion will care. She has proven herself a kindred spirit in the ways of deviancy, and he likes this just fine.

There's a bloom in his belly, and as the bouquet grows, the thorns are tearing up against organs that mean nothing to him. This isn't something as simple as lust. It is more dangerous, and it carries a loathsome weight. He didn't think himself ever capable of experiencing this feeling, but now it creeps up, and Ambrose thinks that it might be impossible to deny.

Is it *love*? Is he truly falling?

What waits for him when he hits bottom?

53

Soulmates

Chat...

PetalsofDandelion: Was it what you imagined?

WatchMeRot: More.

WatchMeRot: So much more. It awoke things.

PetalsofDandelion: What things?

WatchMeRot: Parts I thought mummified. There's always been a black hole in me. This taunting void. Through you, I experienced tiny flashes of light. Thimbles of pleasure in what has always been fallow ground.

PetalsofDandelion: My theory proves true. Not all of you is dead.

WatchMeRot: Don't give me too much credit. My heart remains a charnel house, but where it was once closed, it is now open. You're responsible for that, Dandelion.

PetalsofDandelion: It means a lot that I'm able to inspire you.

WatchMeRot: It's new for me to *feel* like this. I'd be lying to you if I said I wasn't afraid.

PetalsofDandelion: Before I ghosted my therapist a few years back, she used to always tell me that it's best to lean into what you fear. Draw it uncomfortably close until you can literally smell the danger in its pores. That's how you conquer it, and I sense a conqueror in you waiting to be born.

WatchMeRot: You're very supportive. Even to the walking dead.

PetalsofDandelion: Always been a pretty morbid girl.

WatchMeRot: Well since I fear saying this, I suppose it is best to gut it out. I think I love you. I think I've loved you even before I found you. If I am grave dirt, then you are the solitary rose that grows out of it.

PetalsofDandelion: You mean that? With every throbbing scrap of your heart?

WatchMeRot: I do.

PetalsofDandelion: I've been terrified to type it out to you too. I was worried that if I told you, you'd run in the opposite direction. But I feel exactly the same. I've fallen in love with you too, Ambrose. You're in my dreams. I'm drowning and spinning down into the Mariana Trench, but then a decaying hand reaches in to pull me back up to the surface.

PetalsofDandelion: You've saved me. In more ways than you realize, you have saved me.

WatchMeRot: Where do we go from here? I don't know how relationships work. Couples. Romance. It's all alien.

PetalsofDandelion: Anywhere. Everywhere. Even nowhere, as long as we're together.

Dandelion

Usually when she sees herself in the mirror, it is a confrontation. There is judgment and ridicule and a misery that sinks down, deep into the bones. But for the first time in ages, she's admiring her reflection in the bathroom mirror, and she is pleased with what she sees. There is a glow in Dandelion's cheeks, and it's hard for her to stop herself from smiling.

He loves her. He sees her, understands her, and knows her, and at the risk of all things, he still loves her. Dandelion imagines her man's heart floating in a jar of formaldehyde, long discarded and considered useless, but because of her, it thumps again. There is magic in that. If she can awaken love in a man with Cotard's delusion, then surely there must be some part of her that is magic too.

Loud stomps from beyond the door interrupt her daydreams. The smile dies on her lips, and she is quick to bury it. Uncle is home. She's been so consumed with her whirlwind romance with Ambrose that she forgot about him for awhile. He was lurking in the deep, but now he comes again, and he has found her in the shallows.

Uncle is all that is bad in the world. He houses her and provides her with food to eat, but there are unspoken costs. Sweat drips from her temples whenever he's close. The ghost of his rough touch still haunts her, and she subconsciously clenches her thighs together as tightly as humanly possible. The hate she feels for Uncle is radioactive in scale. It burns in her brain and threatens to blot out all rational thought. But with the hate comes stomach-churning fear, and even though she told Ambrose to always face his fear head-on, Uncle is the one creature in her life that she has never been able to overcome.

She doesn't even think of him as a person anymore. When she pictures Uncle in her mind, she sees an anglerfish. Mottled brown skin, an unhinged mouth that gapes low with hooked glass fangs, and a sagging fin protrusion that produces its own infernal blue light. The luminescence comes from a form of biological bacteria, and when the light falls upon her, it makes Dandelion feel sick. She knows that he means to drag her down. He has done it before, and when she's in that deep dark underwater canyon, no one sees her, no one hears the screams, and no one is there to wipe up the sticky blood between her legs when he has satiated his needs for the night.

She stands there breathless in the bathroom, the overhead light flickering, and she can feel his presence on the other side of the door. Looming, hunting, and existing as a walking aberration. The love inside of her is a fragile little flower, and if he catches the scent, he will crush those petals into paste just for fun.

Minutes that feel like eons pass, and then the heavy footfalls transition into another part of the house. Likely the garage, where he'll drink his booze and tinker with his rusted automobiles until a soupy kind of sleep overtakes him.

Dandelion exhales, and the tension in her body starts to fade.

She will not be eaten by the anglerfish tonight. The universe

offers a reprieve. But for a girl like her, how long does lucky

really last?

(Chat...)

WatchMeRot: You seem scattered tonight. Elsewhere.

PetalsofDandelion: I'm good.

WatchMeRot: Are you?

PetalsofDandelion: Fucking peachy. Just a lot on my mind. Sometimes I wish I was born in a different body. Maybe even a different life.

WatchMeRot: What makes you say that?

PetalsofDandelion: Don't interrogate me, Ambrose. I'm just moody. I can't be a good girl all the time. It drains. You're seeing the cracks now. How do you like them?

WatchMeRot: I don't like them.

WatchMeRot: I love them. Every fissure and fracture.

PetalsofDandelion: I'm sorry. You don't deserve my pissy attitude right now. Maybe I should log out until tomorrow.

WatchMeRot: Stay. I think you need me as much as I need you

tonight.

PetalsofDandelion: You don't know everything about me.

That's the benefit of an online persona. I can show you the best

of me while hiding all my worst qualities. There's a literal

demon in my life, for example. I can't escape him.

WatchMeRot: Would you like to tell me about him?

PetalsofDandelion: I will when I'm ready. I promise. But not

yet. Let's savor the fantasies for a little while longer and forget

that anyone else exists.

PetalsofDandelion: What's the most memorable physical

sensation you've ever felt?

WatchMeRot: Well I feel myself rotting on a daily basis, if that

counts. My nostrils are always full of tainted meat.

PetalsofDandelion: I was thinking of another test. A way to

prove that you're not as dead as you believe. Kinda like the

fingernail, but hotter, and maybe a bit worse.

WatchMeRot: Well? Don't leave me in the dark.

PetalsofDandelion: You'll think I'm a freak.

WatchMeRot: I think it's already been established that we both identify with that word.

PetalsofDandelion: Touché.

PetalsofDandelion: My idea involves an open flame.

Ambrose

Ambrose stares down at his exposed genitals, and his examination is dispassionate. It's comparable to a scientist studying a fetal pig. His uncircumcised member is average in size, but the wrinkles on the foreskin make him think of a shy snail that finds solace deep in the shell. This cylinder of meat has long been a forgotten relic in his underwear, but through Dandelion, there has been a resurrection. His cock is Christ rising from the dead, and he'd be lying if he said the thought didn't terrify him.

This foreign object is attached to his body, and it stimulates dormant senses. He's not sure how to process most of them. The experiment Dandelion suggested would likely send a normal man running for the hills, but Ambrose is the opposite of normal. He is the poster child for abnormal, and so he has no issue with entertaining what comes next. In truth, he's deeply curious about the outcome. Is pain the path out of functional

death? Will it make him appreciate existence in a way that he

never has before?

He palms the BIC with his free hand, fingertips teasing at the

spark wheel. She told him ten or twenty seconds should suffice,

but if he is so inclined, there is no limitation on the kiss of flame.

He doesn't know what his threshold is.

He lowers the lighter down next to the head of his shriveled

cock, and he inhales deeply, the aroma of his own rot sitting in

his nostrils. He flicks his wrist, and a baby fire is born. Carefully

he moves the flame downward, allowing it to sizzle against the

head of his dick. There is dim anguish, but it roars in the far back

of his brain, muffled like a zoo animal in a covered cage.

He watches foreskin blister, and then, with seconds ticking

by, there is a crispy blackening. It is a barbecue for one, and he

is the meat. The smell is like sausage drifting through a morning haze, and it cuts through the haunting odor of decay that always lords over him.

There is pleasure in the act. A raw sickly pleasure that shouldn't be there at all, but he cannot deny it. Something repressed and masochistic rattles through him, and his thoughts are full of burning dandelion petals.

Finally, after a brief passage of time, he moves the lighter away from his cock. A tendril of smoke crawls up around his face, providing a halo, and Ambrose feels momentarily angelic. It looks like pork, reddened and ripe, and after a post-burning examination, Ambrose tucks the member back into his underwear.

His nerve endings scream, but he doesn't scream with them. It is nothing to him. A corpse has no reaction to its own cremation. But he wants to make her proud. He wants her to know he did it for her.

He thinks he'd kill the world to kiss her.

Chat...

PetalsofDandelion: I got the picture. You really did it.

WatchMeRot: For you.

PetalsofDandelion: It looks tortured. Ruinous.

WatchMeRot: You approve?

PetalsofDandelion: No man has ever been so devoted to me. When the time comes, I'll lick the scabs off until fresh pink skin shines through.

PetalsofDandelion: Describe the sensation. Spare no detail.

WatchMeRot: It felt good to abuse a part of myself. It felt like taking control for once. I had to remind myself that it was me. Not just some length of sausage cooking on the stovetop.

PetalsofDandelion: It made you feel alive, Ambrose. That is everything. That is animal. You are here, you are real, and you are mine.

WatchMeRot: We own each other now?

PetalsofDandelion: Would you like that? I could wear a collar for you. I'd drink your piss from a doggie dish if you ask me to.

WatchMeRot: I love you so fucking much it burns. I've never had this. I never trusted myself with a pet.

PetalsofDandelion: Why?

WatchMeRot: Always feared that I'd hurt it.

PetalsofDandelion: Sometimes hurt brings people closer together. It bridges the gap.

WatchMeRot: I sometimes think that you've been hurt terribly in your life. I sense it through the screen.

PetalsofDandelion: You're not wrong.

PetalsofDandelion: I am my own sadist, and that has been lonely. I want to share it with someone. We can hurt *together*.

WatchMeRot: I'd like that.

Chat...

WatchMeRot: Do you trust me as I trust you?

PetalsofDandelion: With my life. And with whatever comes after life.

WatchMeRot: There are things I want you to see. Things I saw in my youth holed up in this room to pass the time. The scrapings of human nature. You'll better understand my perception of the world if you do this for me.

PetalsofDandelion: You need only point me in the right direction.

WatchMeRot: It will be uncomfortable. But I think sometimes, under the proper circumstances, discomfort can be a turn-on.

PetalsofDandelion: Yes.

WatchMeRot: I'll send you links. And instructions.

Dandelion

She is back in the abandoned house, her laptop pulling from a mobile hotspot in front of her. Ambrose made it clear that she'd need privacy. She is nude and sitting on a wobbly wooden chair in what remains of a kitchen. Her breasts hang heavy and swollen, nipple clamps firmly attached with a connecting chain between them, per his request. Her vagina is soaked already, and she leaks out on the chair, the nectar of self pooling downward and dribbling against the floor. She's painfully aroused, and her eyes are glazed over as she watches video after video, links sent to her from her man. She is openly weeping, and the tears fall to mix with the juice from her cunt.

The videos are all pulled from the most decrepit corners of the internet. Obscure gore sites, deep web forums, and other nameless online pits of despair. Gangland beheadings with chainsaws. Sledgehammer executions. Three teens beating a homeless man to death with bricks in a wooded area. Violence rolling against violence, all of it stomach churning, but witnessing these atrocities makes Dandelion achingly horny. They shaped Ambrose's upbringing, and in essence, they are a part of him. Everything that is a part of him instills arousal in her.

She imagines him in a lightless room, a dead boy with no friends, watching these gory, fucked-up portholes into the ugliness of humankind. An ice pick into an unconscious lover's soft belly. An obese stalker with his head painted black and red blowing out his own brains on a grainy VHS recording. An emaciated thief in Africa cowering against a rock, one of his hands already amputated as he holds out the other to fiends with machetes, begging them for the opportunity to run after they chop off his other hand so that he can distract himself from the agony.

All the videos blur together, becoming a fetid soup in her mind, and she reaches down and picks up the shattered piece of glass from an old champagne bottle on the floor. Ambrose's instructions were clear for this next part, and she doesn't want to make a mistake. She wants to make it clear who she belongs to. She fantasizes about that stiffening, charbroiled cock of his, and the flood between her thighs only intensifies.

She is carving into her tummy, big messy letters, a jagged phrase of power, and the shard of glass makes little clinking sounds each time it passes across her belly button piercing. Dandelion relishes how it feels, eyes slit, teeth nibbling into bottom lip so hard that it busts, and the entirety of her womanhood leaks out of her to mix together. Blood, tears, and cum, a glimmering pool in this forsaken place, and it will dry and stain long after she's gone.

She admires her handwork before taking a selfie.

HIS WHORE

But only his. No one else can lay claim to her heart or her soul

or her bones. She is *his* gore princess and his alone.

It is a wonderful thing to feel wanted.

Chat...

WatchMeRot: Each letter is a perfect laceration. You did well.

PetalsofDandelion: Really? You don't think my writing looks sloppy?

WatchMeRot: It's beautiful penmanship. If we met during the Civil War, I can only imagine the letters we would have written to each other. Words have always meant a lot to me. Words we share virtually, and words on your flesh.

PetalsofDandelion: Does it ever bother you that our connection is mostly confined to cyberspace?

WatchMeRot: It won't always be. The stars will align for us someday.

PetalsofDandelion: It's hard to believe we were once strangers. Feels like a different life.

WatchMeRot: Speaking of strangers, I've always had to resist the urge to act out against a stranger. To do something unique or awful or bizarre to someone that I don't know and will never see again. It's this itch inside of me. I've never told anyone that, but it feels right to tell you.

PetalsofDandelion: Why resist?

PetalsofDandelion: We could do it together. We might be apart right now, but if we both find someone, we could express ourselves however we wanted. We wouldn't even have to think of them as people. Just mannequins, you know?

WatchMeRot: What are you thinking of doing?

PetalsofDandelion: Let's surprise each other. We'll both find a stranger, and we'll make a toy of them for a little while. Then we report back to each other and compare notes.

WatchMeRot: Sounds fun.

PetalsofDandelion: Yeah. I think it will be.

PetalsofDandelion: Do you ever feel like there's something wrong with us? Almost like there's poison in our souls.

WatchMeRot: We were just born a little different. Poisoned people deserve love and connection too. It's nothing to feel shame over.

PetalsofDandelion: Thank you. It helps to hear that.

Soulmates

Ambrose

Ambrose watches the young woman from afar, making it one of his primary daytime activities. Her routine is habitual, and it rarely deviates. She comes to the same bench in Central Park each morning, a tiny grove beneath a towering oak with roots that burst up from the cobblestone path. There is nothing remarkable about her appearance. Plain face, lank brown hair, and she usually wears burgundy sweaters that are far too big for her.

Her movements are timid and guarded, almost like she's desperate to fade into the background of life. She reminds him of a mouse in human form. It wasn't until week three that he made the realization that she suffers from some form of nonverbal autism. He has watched strangers try to converse with her, and each time it ends awkwardly. She shies away from most social interactions, and for that he cannot blame her.

But while it seems the thought of human companions leads

to indifference for the girl, she absolutely bursts with

enthusiasm when pigeons visit her at the bench. NYC has no

shortage of these brazen sky rats, and if food is involved, they'll

quickly swoop down and feign friendship with the provider. The

girl seems more than happy to give. She brings plastic baggies

full of breadcrumbs, and she encourages the birds to come to

her, relishing the moment when they swarm close and feast at

her feet.

Her smile is a bit crooked, but undeniably sweet. Ambrose

isn't sure of her home situation. He's not sure if she's a runaway,

but she is always alone here. He's never seen her with a

caregiver or guardian of any kind. Her age is indeterminate, but

if pressed, he'd clock her somewhere in her early twenties.

He focuses on the pigeons. He marvels at how genuinely

caring she is to these scavengers. It's like each one is

meaningful to her, and she tries hard to ensure that every visitor gets an equal share of the meal. That fascinates him. Empathy for creatures that are typically shunned or ignored in modern society.

He instantly knows. The girl is his stranger.

***

Ambrose approaches her at the blue hour when the sun is already a sunken remnant on the horizon. Central Park looks hazy and dreamlike at this time of day, and he likes this, because he's here to sell a dream. She won't meet his eyes, gaze downcast, fingers picking at the loose threads on her sleeves. He doesn't bother with words. He shows her a photo album with pictures of large ornate cages on a Midtown rooftop. It looks like a thriving garden, and each cage is a sanctuary for fat and happy pigeons. Eden for birds, and he points to his own chest and mouths that he owns the rooftop garden and the pigeons that call it home. She perks up, eyes growing to the size of saucers. He has captured her attention now.

He doesn't bother to tell her that he pulled the pictures from

a random Instagram post and that his place looks nothing at all

like that. It doesn't matter.

"Wanna see?"

She nods emphatically, head bobbing like a pigeon. He leads

and she follows. They walk for several blocks, and when the

journey takes them down into the subway, the girl never

questions it. She doesn't even seem to notice when the usual

herd of NYC pedestrians disappears as Ambrose navigates to a

desolate subway station that hasn't been used or maintained in

at least seventy years. He scouted it several days before and

found an obscure access tunnel that allows for entry.

It's eerily quiet down there except for the distant rumble of

trains in other locations. No human voices, and no one else to

see. They're surrounded by tiled arches and blacked out

skylights. Ambrose stops dead at a shallow pit of broken tile. It

looks like someone took a pickaxe to the floor and worked hard to create this gash. It's not terribly deep, just a yawning aperture, but it would take a little time and effort for a person to climb up out of it.

The girl walks up next to Ambrose and stares down into the murk, mouth agape. She has a face like the moon, open and round, innocence that rides the razor's edge of gullibility. He softly takes a step back, places a firm hand on her lower back, and pushes the girl in. She has a delayed reaction, a little strangled yelp of surprise that exits her mouth when she hits bottom. It isn't a substantial fall, so only the wind is knocked out of her, but she still looks up at him with an expression of confused shock. It is the look of a dog that openly trusts despite the fact that it has just been kicked in the ribs by its master.

He stares down at her, noting the bits and pieces of gravel and tile in her hair. She's still lying on her back and just managing to push up onto her elbows. Ambrose struggles to feel something for the girl as he looks down at her. He can't summon any tangible emotion. Her face looks slack and dead, just like all the faces he sees, with the exception of Dandelion. This girl's distress doesn't matter. Nothing really matters at all.

He moves over to a large plastic trashcan that he covered with a tarp during his visit here last night. He notices a few feathers and blood speckles around the rim as he uncovers what is within. He carries the heavy trashcan over to the pit, and very gently, he tips it to the side and dumps the contents down on top of the girl.

Fat feathered bodies twitch, squawks of pain drift up, and soon the girl is almost buried up to her neck in a bevy of terrified and mutilated pigeons.

"They can't fly. I clipped their wings with scissors. I cut off their feet with scissors too. But they're alive, and they're with you down there in the dark."

The girl hasn't made a sound yet, but her eyes are darting back and forth like a cornered animal's. There is spittle on her lips and hopeless panic glittering in her gaze.

"It's not personal. It's just a game I'm playing with someone I love. I wasn't sure how you'd react. It made me curious."

Ambrose tilts his head to the side, looking down into the pit inquisitively. The girl seems almost to be swimming against the ruined pigeons, each of them flopping around pathetically, not understanding that they are doomed without feet and flight.

"I suppose I wanted to see if I could make you hate something you once loved. To rewire your brain, you know? You used to associate them with joy. But after this, when you think of pigeons in the future, maybe your feelings will change. Maybe the thought of them will make you want to peel your own skin off. I really don't know. I guess it's not my place to say."

There's certainly no joy in this for Ambrose. It is just something to do. A story to tell Dandelion, and he wants it to be a good one.

"I carved some handholds into the north-facing wall of the pit. It shouldn't take you too long to climb out. You can gather them into your arms and try to take them with you if you like. Maybe try to save them, even though deep down, you know they are broken forever. Death would be better. It usually is."

Ambrose turns from the pit and he starts to walk away. For a good while, there is only the sound of his own footsteps echoing from the rounded walls, but as he reaches the exit, the girl finally finds her voice.

It is a guttural shriek that pierces through him, like a brain straining against something so abhorrent that it's impossible to process, and there is nothing left to do but scream and scream.

The shriek dies away into a sad distant mewling.

Ambrose will never forget the sound. He makes a mental note to describe it to Dandelion in detail.

Dandelion

She spends an entire night canvassing the dive bar, and with last call an hour away, her eyes burn cinders into a target's back. He is large with a pitted face, cheeks colored with good humor. Crew cut, big blonde beard that gives off the scent of cedar even from afar, and large veiny hands that spend most of the night gripping a glass of bourbon. A lonely man from the look of him, some wandering lumberjack seeking a break from the isolation of the woods. The sort of fellow that is a stranger even to himself, and that is what Dandelion wants.

A stranger that never sees it coming. She is feline in her approach, keeping out of his view, soft steps, eyes feral as she creeps up from behind like an ambush hunter. The sound of her body lowering down onto the stool next to him is nothing but a whisper, and it takes him several minutes to realize that she is there.

Just a smile and a twirl of rainbow hair. That's all it takes, and he is none the wiser when her invisible bear trap clamps firmly around his leg. He is tethered to her now, leaning in to catch her words. She's all vague flirtation and doe eyes. She wants him to feel big, strong, and interesting. The masculine of all masculines. The kind of a man that deserves a dainty little girl-thing approaching him in the dead of night when the bar is soon to close.

He tells her he is a logger. He says he spends entire weeks out in nature, not even speaking to another human being. Just crickets and coyotes for company, and after a while, that takes a toll. His only music is the roar of a chainsaw, and each night he lies next to a campfire and counts the stars. There's romanticism in him. Something sentimental about the big lug. That alone will make this better.

"Show me your wilderness."

And so he does. He drives her in his battered pickup along twisty mountain roads, and the headlights cut past low branches and slumbering deer. The journey takes about an hour, give or take. She beams at him the whole way, passenger window slightly cracked so that the wind tousles her hair. He likes her eyes. He says that devils dance in them. If only he knew.

His camp is in a modest clearing near a desolate peak, sequoias lording over them on all sides. She is on him as soon as he lights the campfire, gently mauling. Lips and teeth finding neck, ears, and mouth. She tugs at his skin, nibbling like a kitten, and each little love bite leaves it warm and puckered. He spreads her out on a bed of moss, and when he rips her bra off, the moonlight reflects on the bright pink heart tattoos that decorate both nipples. The shadows are heavy beneath the trees, so the man doesn't even pay attention to the scarred words on her stomach, thinking them just a kinky tattoo.

"Just a little lover girl, aren't you?"

A coquettish nod, and she reaches up to bury her face into his beard, inhaling deeply of the musky aroma. He is in that helpless state that men get into before sex. Lusty, hard, and easily maneuvered. The man is digging a calloused hand into his jeans, telling her that he has a few condoms somewhere, but she playfully shakes her head and directs that huge, calloused paw to her throat instead. Through her constricted windpipe, she gasps out deviancy.

"It's better raw. Like fucking an angel. Pure and pink and pretty. You'll see."

He is speechless, but he does not argue. He's past that now. He is lost in want, and he wants her so fucking bad that it physically hurts. Dandelion wiggles out of her panties and pretends to be shy. She forces him to beg for what she has down there. She feeds him glistening droplets from her fingertips until he is borderline insane. This is power. The pure unfiltered control that comes with womanhood. Hers to wield, and hers to savor.

She lightly kisses his wedding band, making a show of it. This is why she chose him in the bar. It'll make the payoff even better.

"Slide it into me, stranger."

"My name is—"

"Shh. Tonight you have no name. You are flesh and desire, and that is all you are."

When she is finally impaled, it is comparable to demonic possession. Her limbs move in unnatural ways. Her eyes roll, and she growls like a mountain lion over a fresh kill. Dandelion's fingernails dig trenches into the man's back, and it will take them weeks to heal. No hiding the damage she's done. He is so lost in the act that he doesn't realize how many scratches he is bleeding from. He mistakes it for her wetness. Soaked and sinful in the night.

Hours of sex. She is insatiable. Their genitalia become chaffed and bruised after a while, and the union is painful, but it isn't until much later that it stops. When the logger finally rolls off of her and falls asleep, it is a bitter rest that doesn't offer much comfort. He is dehydrated, sore, and covered in patches of poison oak.

Dawn comes far sooner than he'd like, and when his cracked lips open to draw in that first breath of a new day, there is no sign of the young woman that rode him into ruin. Dandelion is gone, clothes and all. She must have taken off on foot, and it won't take her a terribly long time to reach town.

There is a giant piece of sequoia bark propped up against the hood of his truck. Words have been carved into it with a discarded pocketknife. The man stumbles forward and squints through the sunshine.

"I forgot to tell you. If you notice a few red spots down there soon, don't worry, it is just genital herpes. I should also disclose

to you that I am HIV positive. Thank you for a wonderful evening ☺"

The man freezes in place. His teeth grit together, impotent rage causing his entire frame to tremble. He smashes a fist down against the hood of the truck and manages to break his thumb in the process.

Somewhere far away on a game trail that leads down the mountain, Dandelion's laughter mixes with birdsong. Satisfied with her lie, she cannot wait to get home and message Ambrose about her experience.

Chat...

PetalsofDandelion: You have to be shitting me. You cut the feet off pigeons?

WatchMeRot: I did.

WatchMeRot: There was no pleasure in the butchery. It just had to be done for the experiment to carry any weight.

PetalsofDandelion: You're diabolical, Ambrose. Truly. I have to admit I'm impressed. What sound do pigeons make when you cut them up? Do they scream?

WatchMeRot: Not nearly as loudly as the girl did.

PetalsofDandelion: I wonder what she was thinking down there buried up to her neck.

WatchMeRot: Hard to say. She was just a stranger. I never got to know her well enough to figure it out.

WatchMeRot: Tell me about yours.

PetalsofDandelion: He was big. Brawny. I met him in a bar.

Hard to forget his eyes. They seemed full of kindness and conflict all at the same time.

PetalsofDandelion: Struck me as one of those married guys that is away from home for long periods. So lonesome. So lost. I think if I hadn't pressed the issue, he would have remained loyal.

WatchMeRot: What did you do to him?

PetalsofDandelion: Oh honey, what didn't I do. We went to the woods. I seduced him. I made him putty, and it's never been hard to turn a man to putty. We fucked. I think he came inside of me, because it was dribbling down my thighs when I left the camp the next morning.

PetalsofDandelion: I had to scrub my hands in the sink for a long time after because I had chunks of his skin under my fingernails. I tore him up. I imagine his woman will wonder about those scars for many years after. What caused them. What kind of animal wounded him so.

PetalsofDandelion: I left him a lie. A note about having a few especially nasty and stress-inducing STDs. Don't worry, it was all fiction, but I'm sure it had the intended effect. I wanted it to build a beehive in his brain. What do you think?

WatchMeRot: Rewind a bit. You said you fucked him?

PetalsofDandelion: Well yeah, babe, but it didn't mean anything at all. I felt nothing for that husk. It was all part of our game.

WatchMeRot: I thought you loved me.

PetalsofDandelion: I do love you! Achingly. With everything that I am. He was a toy. He was disposable meat. You get that, right?

PetalsofDandelion: Did I make a mistake here?

WatchMeRot: I don't like that you did that. You were with a man full of life and vitality. How will I compare when the time comes? Can the cock of a corpse even satisfy you?

PetalsofDandelion: You're not a corpse, Ambrose. You're so much more than that. Maybe this was a misstep. Maybe I got carried away with the game.

PetalsofDandelion: Can we chalk it up to a spur of the moment accident? You can forgive that, right?

WatchMeRot: I'm signing off for the night.

Ambrose

Ambrose sits in a tattered recliner, not a single bit of illumination in the room aside from a flat screen that broadcasts white noise. He's trying to self-soothe by staring into the static void, but it isn't working. His heart is full of worms, and they bedevil him. He can't stop picturing Dandelion lost in the act of passion with another man. The toss of her sweat-soaked rainbow hair, the biting of her lips, and the grind of hips that he thought were meant for him alone.

When the game of strangers was agreed to, he never thought it would go in this direction. It feels like a betrayal. It feels like she planted seeds inside of him, allowed them to bloom, and then clipped the growth before he ever learned how to properly flourish. Dead, resurrected, and then dead again.

He rises from the recliner and approaches the TV. He is stoic for several moments before leaning forward and planting his boot into the screen as hard as he can. It bursts into spiderweb cracks and falls, and he lifts the boot up high and stomps repeatedly downward, relishing the crunch under his heel. If someone were there to witness it, they wouldn't see uncontrollable fury boiling outward. This is cold and precise violence, and there is something robotic about the movements. But the rage exists in his chest, a hidden furnace that he never knew could flame up so drastically. It is an unfamiliar emotion, yet another new feeling that Dandelion has awoken in the shell that he used to be.

When he is done, he stands there, taking in clipped shallow breaths, and he reaches up to slick his hair back across his scalp. There must be retaliation.

***

A life of relative isolation and bedroom rotting has made Ambrose very skilled with computers. Dandelion named the bar for him, so it's easy to pinpoint the location. It's more complex to hack into the lone parking lot surveillance camera and scroll back through the grainy footage from the night of Dandelion's adventure.

It doesn't take him long to find the man walking into the bar. A big brutish thing with wide shoulders and logging equipment in the bed of his truck. Luck smiles on Ambrose, because there is a clear picture of the man's license plate. He runs the numbers, and he's able to find a residence in Oregon.

He has no plans to visit the man directly, although it is a tempting thought. Instead, he hunts down the contact information of a trusted relative on social media, and he forges a card to the best of his abilities. He drops the care package off in the mail the next day.

Oatmeal cookies, known to be the man's favorite according to a comment he left on a YouTube cooking video in 2009. He hopes that the parcel arrives safely.

He doubts the man will notice the taste of strychnine in the batch, because it was mixed in lovingly with other normal ingredients. A delectable treat for a woman-stealing rat.

When it is done, Ambrose feels better. The threat has been handled. Surely Dandelion meant no lasting harm against him.

He decides it is best to forgive.

Dandelion

Her throat is raw from crying, and mascara has bled down from her eyes to create black tentacles on her cheeks. She fucked up righteously. It felt lighthearted and only a little devious to her in the moment. Sex has always had that association in her mind. Something playful and low stakes to dive into whenever she is bored, but Ambrose doesn't see it that way. She sensed genuine hurt as he was messaging her, and the thought of her man hurting makes her want to hurt herself.

She's been doing that for the last hour. Dandelion balls up her fist and smashes it into her temple for the eighth time, and the repeated blows have caused a purple, orchid-shaped bruise to spread outward from her brow. So goddamn idiotic. A worthless little slutbaby that humps before she thinks. It's possible that she has messed this up forever. Her soulmate is upset, and she doesn't know how to fix it. She can't unfuck the lumberjack. How to make this right?

She's sitting on the porch and listening to stray cats fight each other somewhere out in the night. If she could see them, she'd hiss right back at the felines. She is furious and devastated, and she has no one to blame but herself. Endless guilt. So much guilt that she chokes on it while she sits there in her pathetic, blubbering state.

Snot drips down from her nose, and she doesn't have the strength to wipe it away. Her hair is an unwashed mess, and she put it up into ratty pigtails because she didn't know what else to do with it. There's a moth that keeps suicide-diving into the dome light on the porch, and she understands completely how the doomed creature feels.

The slow creak of hinges as the screen door opens. Dandelion's body goes into fight-or-flight mode. But she chooses neither option. She freezes like a rabbit, and she begins to tremble despite that fact that it isn't cold. Her mind retreats into a dim nothing-place. Dandelion thinks of it as her own personal midnight zone. A realm so deep and sable and hopeless in the ocean, just pitch-black pressure and the quiet rumble of underwater volcanic vents. There is an anglerfish circling, and it brings with it an appetite that she is all too familiar with.

Powerful hands with illegible knuckle tattoos descend and clamp across her shoulders, making her feel birdlike and fragile. She is facing the yard and Uncle is behind her. She doesn't have to look at him, and that is a small mercy. It was already shaping up to be a bad night. Now she is assured of a hell-night. Her thoughts break apart in her head and become marine snow, just floating detritus in the void.

He smells like sin and cigarettes. He is an untreated wound, and he likes to fester. She feels him leaning down against her, and when he speaks, she is already in the process of drowning.

"Rent is due."

Dandelion closes her eyes and silently hyperventilates.

Chat...

PetalsofDandelion: Hello?

PetalsofDandelion: You hate me, don't you?

WatchMeRot: I took some time to reflect. I don't hate you, Dandelion.

WatchMeRot: Is it safe to say you did this with no malice in your heart? You didn't intend to hurt me, right?

PetalsofDandelion: Never. If I had the option to fling myself into oncoming traffic or break your heart, then I would gladly let the tires of an eighteen wheeler turn me to gristle.

PetalsofDandelion: I'm so fucking sorry for what happened. I have weird views on sex because of my upbringing. I thought you'd see it as me just fucking with that guy so that I'd have a good story for you. I wanted it to be memorable. Something you'd laugh over.

WatchMeRot: Water under the bridge. I forgive you. But never again, Dandelion. Your slit belongs to me. All of you does. The body is sacred, and I want no other person on this planet to have access to you.

PetalsofDandelion: Yes, Daddy. A whore for you and no other.

WatchMeRot: It's been a week. How are you?

PetalsofDandelion: I want to lie, Ambrose. I want to tell you I'm okay. I've missed you. There are more holes in me than you realize, and you fill each one of them up.

PetalsofDandelion: Remember that problem I mentioned a while back? That demon that is deeply rooted in my life. It's been getting worse. It's my Uncle.

PetalsofDandelion: He hurts me. He uses me. He takes parts of me that I never offer him. And I feel like it'll never get better. It's hard to see the light when he always drags me back into the dark.

WatchMeRot: What does he do to you?

PetalsofDandelion: I don't want to rehash it, but you can guess. He takes his pounds of flesh. I try to disassociate when it happens. My mind drifts far away, and it doesn't float back until he's left me bleeding and crying on the floor.

PetalsofDandelion: I hate him more than anything. But I am terrified of him. He is larger than life in my thoughts. I've never figured out how to protect myself from him.

WatchMeRot: I'll protect you.

WatchMeRot: You gave me life when I thought it wasn't possible. If it wasn't for you, I'd walk into the funeral home and ask for an early burial.

PetalsofDandelion: But how?

WatchMeRot: Together. That's how we win. We plot. It'll be like our last game, but with new rules.

WatchMeRot: You do not deserve the things he does to you. But he deserves what we will do to him. Uncle has earned his reckoning.

PetalsofDandelion: You give me hope. I haven't had much hope in my life.

WatchMeRot: For this to work, we have to truly be together. Not just on the internet. I'll need to leave New York and travel to Oregon.

PetalsofDandelion: And we'd get to meet face to face for the first time ever. I've dreamed of that moment.

WatchMeRot: Well, dreams do come true.

(Chat...)

PetalsofDandelion: It's a long trip. I worry about you.

WatchMeRot: Coast to coast. A lot of miles between here and there. It doesn't matter. Even if you were in Antarctica, I'd find a way.

PetalsofDandelion: Will you drive?

WatchMeRot: Never learned. I grew up in NYC. Child of the subway. Been riding those big subterranean worms my entire life. A strange way of travel if you think about it. So normalized to pack yourself into a space with other stinking humans and rattle through the underground.

WatchMeRot: But there are Greyhounds, trains, and even the will to hitchhike if I get desperate enough. I've never been out west. What's Oregon like?

PetalsofDandelion: Mild and cool mostly. We get a lot of rain.

It's easy for people to lose themselves in all the rain. It can be

boring.

PetalsofDandelion: But all that aside, what do we do here,

Ambrose? What's your plan for him?

WatchMeRot: We kill him.

PetalsofDandelion: I've never done anything like that. I don't

know if I can kill a person. And what about prison? All those

shitty consequences that can come after.

WatchMeRot: We'll do it quick and quiet, and no evidence will

remain. And then we'll disappear. We'll fade into the fog and no

one will even remember our names.

PetalsofDandelion: Don't you have any family that will miss

you?

WatchMeRot: I renounced most of my blood connections long

ago. As far as they're concerned, I am dead already.

WatchMeRot: I've never killed anyone either if you can believe it. I have done bad things. Inflicted great harm on those deserving of it. But even though there has been hurt, I don't think that I've ever succeeded in murdering anyone.

PetalsofDandelion: What about that rat poison you said you sent to the logger?

WatchMeRot: It was a low enough dose to make him violently ill, but if he gets the proper care, he'll live. It was to be a horrible lesson, but a lesson meant to be survived.

PetalsofDandelion: So this will be a first for both of us. Like popping our cherries when it comes to ending a life. It's something we can't take back. The stakes are higher in comparison to the other lines we have crossed together.

WatchMeRot: You want this, don't you? You want it to stop with Uncle. You want him to release the control he has over you. This is how we accomplish that.

PetalsofDandelion: Yes please. And I don't want to rush you, but I hope it can be soon. He's been worse lately. It's like he has some gut instinct that things are about to change.

WatchMeRot: Oh, they are.

WatchMeRot: I'll come as fast as I can.

Dandelion

Dandelion stands at the refrigerator and carefully selects blueberries from a container, popping several into her mouth at once and savoring the burst of flavor. She wants to keep her strength up, because she'll need it for when Ambrose arrives. The nerves already thrum in her like a live wire, and she's so preoccupied with her own ruminations that she doesn't hear Uncle arrive until it's too late.

A hand snakes around her ponytail and smashes her face into the front of the freezer door, the impact stunning her and causing her nose to leak blood like a faucet. She didn't hear the telltale crunch of it breaking, but it feels busted and inflamed nevertheless. Uncle boxes her in, his big sweaty body pressing intimately close to her and wedging her spine-first against the fridge. A calloused hand rises and clamps around her throat, thumb biting into her chin as he lifts her head up so she's forced

to look at him.

"You seem distracted lately. Eyes shifty and hard to read. I

don't much care for that."

He digs his fingers deep into her hair and wrenches her neck

painfully to the side, relishing the little hiss of discomfort that

escapes her lips. Uncle shreds the thin material of the tank top

she's wearing, and she is powerless to stop it. A red blush of

shame creeps across the upper portions of her breasts.

"Don't lose sight of your role here. I've been charitable with

you. Sometimes I feel like the gratitude isn't really there, ya

know?"

He stares her up and down, awaiting a response. Dandelion

gulps and lets her gaze flit over him. Her mind scrubs his human

features away as a coping mechanism, and all she sees are giant

bulbous silver-colored eyes, clear needle fangs, and a strobing bioluminescence that nearly blinds her. The anglerfish is unhappy, and its jaws gape wide.

"I am grateful. Thank you for everything. All that you've done for me."

She barely gets it out without gasping, and Uncle moves her slightly to the side and opens the freezer. He retrieves a tray of ice cubes and snatches a single one up into his grasp, and he throws the rest of the tray back over his shoulder. There's a loud clattering as ice cubes skate around all over the kitchen floor.

He begins to scrub the ice cube against both of Dandelion's nipples, a slicing sensation that leaves her feeling raw and exposed. Uncle is open with his vulgarity, and his mannerisms make her skin crawl.

"Whatever has you so riled up? Let's cool it down, lil' flower. Don't get too stuck in your head, because I will beat that pretty head against the fridge until your brain looks like scrambled eggs if you keep your shit up. We crystal?"

She nods, eyes huge and rimmed with tears, and Uncle slowly lifts up his hand and motions for her to open her mouth. She slides out a quivering tongue, as has been his expectation of her many times, and he gently deposits the melting ice cube into her mouth. Rough fingers manipulate her chin and lift it up, closing her mouth in the process.

"Swallow that down. And cool off."

She tries her best, throat working, but the ice cube is painful and scratchy as it slides down her esophagus. She starts choking and coughing, and he slings her to the side and beats her companionably on the back until the fit starts to dissipate.

Uncle has already started to wander off in the direction of the living room. He often grows bored of her after a random torture session, and Dandelion is left there in a state of borderline hysteria with a ripped shirt and beads of water dripping down her chest.

"I'll expect to smell dinner cooking on that stove in the next hour."

The threat has passed, but the trauma deepens. She grabs a wad of paper towels and does her best to blot up the plasma crusted around her nose.

She wills her prince to get here before it's too late.

Ambrose

Bleak, gray morning hours from the window of the Greyhound, Ambrose's forehead pressing against the glass as he watches the seemingly endless rainfall. He's somewhere in Ohio, and there is nothing much to see. Darkness still clings to the world, and it is reluctant to roll aside for the daylight.

It's deathly still on the bus, his fellow passengers barely stirring at this time. He catches a whiff of a few foul aromas, but the lack of hygiene is not unusual during a long bus trip. It's no worse than the scent of his own rotten skin and the grubs that burrow through his intestines. His gaze floats across grizzled faces obscured by hoods and baseball caps pulled down low. Lost souls that want to get somewhere, even if it means they have to travel through nowhere.

He struggles to feel some level of sentimentality for them. He cannot. They are livestock in a universal slaughterhouse, and most of them are too stupid to realize it. There is no glow in them, not even a spark of light. Dim bulbs with shattered interiors. Dandelion is the exact opposite. She is the sun. Her rays stimulate and awaken. When her attention falls across his dead pores, he bends towards her like a weed that has been denied for decades.

There is only one Dandelion on this planet. He is assured of the fact that he will never encounter another like her for the remainder of his days in this half-life limbo that imprisons him. Ambrose has one chance at love, to experience it as normal people do, and he is willing to risk it all for that. The sad little thimble of meat he calls a heart sings for closeness with this woman.

But just like a knight in an old fantasy novel, if the woman is to be won, a monster must be slain. He can't imagine what Uncle is like. He pictures something large and veiny and warped by taboo appetites. The demon is crafty to have hidden in plain sight for this long, and Ambrose knows it won't be the easiest

task in the world to put him down. But he is motivated. He

wants what he wants, and he means to have her.

Chat...

PetalsofDandelion: Where are you?

WatchMeRot: Somewhere in Ohio. We're moving slow.

PetalsofDandelion: He bounced my head off the fridge last night. Choked me. Did other things I don't want to mention.

WatchMeRot: I'm so sorry. Just know that I am coming, and it will stop.

PetalsofDandelion: It's nothing new. I'm used to it. But everything about this makes me anxious.

PetalsofDandelion: It's ridiculous to say, but it's like he smells you on me. Senses what we have in store for him. He's been unsettled, way more unpredictable than I'm accustomed to. Usually it's just ugly words and the uglier pleasures he throws my way. His violence is evolving.

WatchMeRot: Can you do your best to avoid him? Make yourself scarce. Just a little mouse in the house.

PetalsofDandelion: I'll try.

PetalsofDandelion: Are we really going to do what you said we're going to do?

WatchMeRot: Yes.

WatchMeRot: The more you tell me about him, the more I want to.

PetalsofDandelion: I really love you. I feel like some part of me summoned you from a cold dark place in time. When I needed you the most, you know?

WatchMeRot: When it's over, you can smear his blood on me. It might make me warm for you. More appropriate when kissing a cadaver.

PetalsofDandelion: I'll make you warm even if it's the last thing I do. How far now? How long?

WatchMeRot: Still far. But inching my way across the fathoms. I know you can feel me getting closer.

WatchMeRot: Hang in a little longer. When the nightmare ends,

the dream begins.

Ambrose

It is after midnight somewhere in the green sea of Nebraska. Ambrose has been looking at corn for hours, and he's starting to think that nothing else exists but those tall stalks swaying slowly in the breeze. The bus has stopped briefly to allow the passengers to stretch their legs. They mostly herd in loose groups across the road, smoking their cigarettes and not saying much of anything to one another. He is apart from them, and that isn't unusual for him.

Ambrose stands by himself on the opposite side of the desolate road, facing a cornfield that dominates the flat horizon for as far as he's able to see. The sky is painfully clear, and there are too many stars. There is wind, but it's subtle, little more than a whisper as it passes through the husks.

A man materializes in front of Ambrose. He detaches himself from the corn stalks and simply stands there, bathed in their shadow. It's hard to discern features. He wears a black suit and a black wide-brimmed hat on his head. His face is downcast so that nothing shows but a jawline shaped like a sickle of moon.

"Do you think the journey is worth it?"

Ambrose shuffles his feet and cocks his head at the man.

"Long miles and longer nights. And of course, the longing in you. That must also be calculated."

"I've got a good reason to get where I'm going."

"A woman, huh? Few can deafen their ears to that kind of siren song. We've all been there. Heart beats a little faster. Sweat in the pits and on the temples. It is brave to risk your heart. Some live their entire lives and never do."

"What do you know about me, stranger?"

"I know you have sat in your loneliness for longer than most would be able to endure. Stiffness in your limbs, and when you brush your teeth, you always taste embalming fluid. There's this sickly sweet death smell that is with you wherever you go.

Others don't smell it, but you do. I know there have been days

where you have willed your own bed to be six feet under so that

you don't have to pull yourself up out of it to face civilization.

Am I right about all that?"

Ambrose just stares. He is not afraid, but the man's presence

makes no sense. He knows things he has no business knowing.

"You're dead only in your own mind, but that is enough. It is

a burden all its own. Can she love someone like you? Can't she

find better? A partner that savors life. They're everywhere in this

world. Every person is a season. Most people are spring. They're

growing and alive, and they relish the bloom."

The man fetches a soft sigh, and he brushes a thumb across

the brim of his hat.

"I see winter in you. Bare branches and a bare soul. The

leaves fell, dead. The flowers dried up. The soil got hard and

cold, and it's almost impossible to pierce now. Months of

stillness, months of nights at their darkest. That is what you bring to the table. Can she ever be satisfied with that?"

"Show me your face."

The man steps forward and thrusts his features into moonlight. There really isn't a face to be seen. It is all decaying soup, maggots in sunken sockets, and strips of skin clinging to stained, horse-like teeth. Even so, Ambrose finds the face recognizable. He abhors mirrors, but he has glimpsed the face a time or two before. His reflection of shame. Like Dorian Gray's portrait, it is best not to look.

"The bus is leaving soon. Don't miss it."

Ambrose blinks, and there is no man in front of him. There was a little hissing sound like the helium leaving a balloon, and then he just popped out of existence. All that remains is corn and the wind that teases through the stalks.

Ambrose turns around and heads back to board the bus. The man in the black hat is wrong. Dandelion welcomes the winter, and he will not be dissuaded.

Dandelion

She purchased a hog's head from the local butcher shop, and now she's lugging it through the woods in a brown paper bag. It's far heavier than she anticipated, and she has broken out in a sweat, hair clumped and dripping around her head. Her makeup runs in the most unflattering way possible and she doesn't even bother trying to fix it.

She finds a tiny dead tree that's just a foot shorter than her, and she pulls the head from the bag and jams it down on the ragged stump until it's deeply impaled. The hog stares at her with milky dead eyes and a lolling tongue. A few bloated, green flies circle around it, and they sample the slack pink meat with their proboscises.

Dandelion read somewhere online that pigs have a similar anatomy to humans. She takes a deep breath and pulls a steak knife out from her sock. It feels clunky in her hand, and she's afraid she'll slip and slice up her own fingers. She's usually very

comfortable around a blade if she is using it to harm her own

body, but when comes to the thought of stabbing another

person, she is a fish out of water. Her mind swims with

uncertainty and insecurity. How much pressure to apply? What

slashing angle to inflict a fatal wound?

She's all alone out here. There's an owl hooting somewhere

over the next ridge, but that's the only company she has. No one

to judge. She uses that thought to reaffirm her choice, and she

darts forward and slashes the knife downward. It's an awkward

attack, and it serves only to flay open the hog's cheek. She tries

again, thrusting upward while letting out an emotional shriek,

but the blade grazes against the bark of the tree and barely even

penetrates the hog's neck.

She reaches forward to yank it free from the flesh, and in her

enthusiasm, her legs tangle together and she falls awkwardly to

her side, the knife clattering down against a few lichen-covered rocks. The hog's head is looming over her, almost seeming to mock her paltry efforts. She sees Uncle watching from those milky dead eyes. How will it be when this is for real? No take backs and no practice shots.

Before she even realizes it, she is ugly-crying. The self-doubt feels like a weight in her belly. This man has tormented her for years. He has made her feel like the smallest speck of shit in the entire universe. He will kill her, and he will not hesitate. Her fingers tremble from genuine terror. It's one thing to talk about being free of him, but taking action is entirely different.

She wants to bury herself in the crunchy brown leaves and never surface again. She wants to hide. If she's being fully honest with herself, a part of Dandelion has been hiding for her entire life.

Chat...

PetalsofDandelion: I don't think I can do this.

WatchMeRot: You can. You *must*.

PetalsofDandelion: I practiced with a knife. It was embarrassing. Just the thought of actually sticking it into another person makes me nauseous.

WatchMeRot: Oh darling, we've done more daring things than that to each other. It'll slide in like butter. You won't even notice the difference.

WatchMeRot: I will teach you.

PetalsofDandelion: I trust you. I'm just feeling really jittery. Hyping it up in my head, you know?

WatchMeRot: When the time comes, I'll hold your hand. It'll help you get through it.

Ambrose

Wyoming passes in a blur of emptiness and snow-capped peaks. The Bighorn Mountains loom large through the windows of the bus, and Ambrose imagines how many millions and millions of years it took for the land to form those jagged teeth. It's that bright yellow time in the evening when the sunlight threatens to burn your eyeballs right out of the sockets if you look at it directly. The intense glare is probably why the bus driver never even notices the elk.

It is a huge, majestic beast, and Ambrose only catches a brief glimpse of eyes and antlers before the Greyhound splatters it into gore. There's a hideous crunch as biological material collides with metal, and the front of the bus crumples inward like a tin can. The driver is mashed into an unrecognizable rag doll in a matter of moments. The bus skids sideways across the road and comes to a stop next to the tree line. Most of the passengers are crawling along the floor, dazed, and others

smacked their heads against hard surfaces and now sit slumped

unconscious in their seats.

Ambrose was lucky. The impact rattled him, but he clung to

his seat and weathered the storm. He's staring up at the torn

crater where the front of the bus used to be. The elk is nearly

sliced clean in two, mangled body halfway through the

windshield. By some dark miracle, the animal is still alive. It

bleats mournfully as it bleeds out, and it tosses that heavy head

from side to side, enormous antlers smashing up against seats

and passengers in equal measure.

There are a few people fighting with the escape hatch

leading to the roof, but it's jammed against a massive tree limb,

and the fight is getting them nowhere. Ambrose seems to be the

only one who notices the exposed wiring that is sending out

sparks near the elk. It doesn't take long for leaking fuel beneath the bus to ignite, and then the flames rise and threaten to consume. The world is smoke, fire, and screams.

The people that remain inside are panicked sardines, all trying to avoid being cooked alive. Ambrose is the only one who keeps his head. His heartbeat is placid and unbothered, and despite the chaos, he remains pragmatic.

He notices that his window is shattered. It's the only one in the entire bus that busted outward during the crash. No one else notices. They're lost in the smoke and the bleating. He lifts his torso and snakes his arms out of the open window, and he pulls himself out with relative ease. This side of the bus hasn't yet succumbed to the inferno, so he's able to drop down and roll to the side. He is free.

He could call someone. He could report the accident and have police and EMS en route within minutes. Instead of doing any of those things, he just stands there and watches impassively as the Greyhound burns. The air smells of sausages and elk piss. Melting faces watch him from the blackening windows, fists slamming, eyes saucer-like with pain and fear, all of them begging him to do something. One old woman's hair is on fire, and when she presses her cheek against the hot glass of a window, her skin sloughs downward like boiled plastic.

There really isn't much left to see. The people are dead already. They've always been dead, this moment just makes them aware of the fact. Ambrose turns his back on them and walks down the highway. This is an inconvenience, but he will not be deterred.

He'll cover what remains of the trip to Oregon on foot if he has to.

Chat...

PetalsofDandelion: What's your ETA?

WatchMeRot: There were complications. But I'm not far. I've made it to Idaho.

PetalsofDandelion: You're only one state away from me now. It's hard to believe this is real.

PetalsofDandelion: I keep thinking I'm going to wake up at some point and realize that the bond we've forged was just an elaborate dream.

WatchMeRot: You'll see that I'm real enough when you wrap your arms around me.

WatchMeRot: Are you safe?

PetalsofDandelion: For now. I keep thinking I should crush up sleeping pills and put them into his beer so that he's lethargic when you get here. But I don't know how to calculate the dosage, and a part of me is really scared to try.

WatchMeRot: When the time comes, we'll wing it.

PetalsofDandelion: What do you think it'll be like when we're face to face? What if my tongue gets all twisted and I can't find the right words?

WatchMeRot: That's alright. Our souls will talk.

PetalsofDandelion: Soulmates until the end?

WatchMeRot: Until the end.

Dandelion

Her anxiety has been at an all-time high, so she's trying to distract herself with yoga. She's doing downward-facing dog when her bedroom door explodes open. The work boot snaps into her ribs with maximum force, and she flies across the room and tumbles down against the hardwood floor. She tries to push up and get her bearings, but he's on her in a matter of minutes, and his kicks find her torso over and over, the toe of his boot digging into her skin with enough force to leave massive bruising.

Dandelion is finding it hard to get her wind back, and Uncle mashes his heel down against her thigh, grinding his boot back and forth to emphasize his point. Her room is all dim lamplight, so she can barely see his expression, but he's leaning down and shoving one of her spiral notebooks into her face. It's open to a page full of black hearts and doodles centered around Ambrose's name.

"When I saw how you scratched those letters into yourself, you told me you did that for me. I smelled the lie then, and now the stink of it is overwhelming. 'His whore,' huh? *Ambrose's* whore?"

She's weakly pawing against his boot, trying to appease his anger enough to allow for an explanation, but he responds by stomping down directly on her abdomen and causing a wave of pain to travel through her stomach. She turns her head awkwardly to the side and closes her eyes, hoping against all hopes that she doesn't vomit in front of him.

"You've been playing on that internet again. I've caught you before. Talking nasty with boys. Showing yourself. You've got a new crush, and you thought you'd hide him from me."

Uncle reaches down and buries his fist into her hair, and he starts to drag her by the roots across the floor. She flops from side to side, trying to dig her fingernails into the floor, but there's no purchase to be found. She keeps attempting to articulate the word "please," but her body feels pulverized by the kicks, and it's hard to find the strength to speak above a whisper.

"That stops tonight. You won't be eating the next few days. You need time to think. We'll let that regret and remorse settle in, won't we? And when those hunger pangs start hitting and you get tired of staring at the walls, you remember who owns you."

Uncle reaches down and picks her up like she weighs nothing, and he moves in the direction of the narrow attic door. It's always kept padlocked because there's a rat infestation up there, but he wastes no time in inserting the key and throwing the door open. Dandelion is slumped over one of his bony shoulders, and he tosses her onto the staircase unceremoniously. New anguish lights her up as the sharp edges of the stairs dig into her already brutalized form. She can barely lift her head and gaze balefully at him from behind a curtain of sweat-drenched hair.

"I spent plenty of time in solitary confinement in my younger days. It builds character. You'll find that out the hard way. Let's see who you really are, girl."

The door slams shut, and the anglerfish is gone. She listens as the padlock is reaffixed into place. It's stifling hot up here in the attic, not much to see but dusty boxes and insulation curling down in tatters from the thick wooden beams.

Dandelion barely manages to push her body up against the wall into a sitting position, and the true nature of her predicament forces her into hopelessness. She lifts trembling hands and covers up her face, not wanting to see even a small glimpse of this vindictive fucking world that she inhabits.

She is cut off from Ambrose for the moment, and that is worst of all. It feels like the loss of a limb. The excision of her heart.

The sudden absence aches more than the rest of her.

Dandelion

She winces and rolls over, proceeding to crawl across the ragged floorboards. Her entire body feels like tenderized meat, and it wouldn't surprise her if her ribs were busted up. Pairs of beady, black, oil-drop eyes watch her from nests of insulation, but the rats do not show themselves now that an intruder is in their midst.

Dandelion tears apart dusty boxes and pushes old forgotten relics of furniture to the side. She has no idea what she's looking for, but the heat of the attic is giving her a massive migraine, and she needs to distract herself. If there's an old cellular phone or something up here that she can use to connect to the Wi-Fi and contact Ambrose, then a sliver of hope exists.

Her breathing is labored and clipped, and the smell of rodent feces is driving her mad. She stumbles to the side while clamping her nostrils shut, and completely by accident, she pushes a stack of thick drapery to the side, and underneath is a mahogany desk. There is a fossil of a desktop PC sitting on the surface, screen scrummed over with dust, keyboard partially broken and missing letters, but if she can somehow get this artifact to connect to the home Wi-Fi, then a cry for help is possible.

She begins to frantically wipe dust and cobwebs aside in clawing motions, and when she plugs the computer in and crosses her fingers, a muffled shriek of joy escapes her lips as the screen brightens up. There's still some juice left in it, and she can work with that.

She feels like a wounded princess locked in a tower, and now is the time to send out a raven.

Hopefully the message reaches the intended recipient.

Chat...

PetalsofDandelion: please come. come quick.

PetalsofDandelion: am locked in attic. bruised and weak. he knows about you.

PetalsofDandelion: i am scar ed. bring knives or gun or something. he wont let me out.

WatchMeRot: I am so sorry, Dandelion. I'm almost there.

WatchMeRot: I am going to rip him apart.

Ambrose

It is night in Gearhart, Oregon, and it is night inside of him. The final miles were accomplished through hitchhiking and a stolen bicycle, but after a journey that has left him feeling like a ragged wanderer, Ambrose stands at the threshold of everything that he has ever wanted.

The sea churns violently to his left, and the cliffs are like claws that cradle the sagging Victorian extra close. It is just how Dandelion described it. An inherited house that was once beautiful, but a lifetime of neglect from Uncle has left it looking like a shadow of its former self. There is light in a few of the windows, winking and ephemeral, and it's hard to tell if anything is up and about. It's especially late, and he planned his approach at this exact hour when the entire world is deathly quiet.

His eyes flit up to the attic. There is only one blacked out window up there, and nothing at all to be seen, but he *feels* her. This warm pulsing presence like bright yellow petals unfurling and beckoning onward. Empathy sparks in his heart, and he doesn't understand the emotion because of how foreign is to him. It constricts Ambrose's facial features and twists them with a yearning that is greater than himself.

His gaze doesn't linger long on the attic. It moves down to drink in the larger structure of the house. All that it represents. A den for a brute. A cave for a fiend. A shell for a merciless crustacean that feeds without thought. It is mockingly close, and he feels that too.

Dead cells twitch in his skin. Long-dormant internal volcanoes erupt and threaten to spill over. The cadaver that he was shakes off the grave dirt of a previous life, and it crawls to the surface, gasping for air. He glowers, and a storm gathers behind his irises. His hand snakes down into his brown leather satchel and lovingly caresses the awl that is hidden in there. The wooden handle and the razor-tipped sharpness of the point.

Ambrose understands how Lazarus felt now. This is resurrection. She has called, and he has come. Dandelion is behind those walls, and she needs him now more than ever.

The hate that he feels in this moment is more powerful than anything that he has ever felt in his entire life.

He intends to use it.

Ambrose lowers his shoulders and strides in the direction of fate.

Dandelion

The rats start to get more brazen after sundown. She sits slumped against the wall, watching them scurry down from the insulation, noses twitching, eyes blackly curious, and so much of their sly attention is focused on her. Dandelion is weeping silently, tears moist on her cheeks. She wants to sleep but she doesn't dare. She's afraid she will awaken to them covering her and nibbling at her exposed skin.

And to make matters worse, there is noise from the attic door. It's a metallic grinding, and she has no idea what new psychological method Uncle is using to torment her. Her hands are clamped over her ears, but it doesn't do much good. Soon she will have to push off the wall and stand on spaghetti legs. She'll have to lift up weakened fists and try to fight off his malice. She knows in her heart that she will lose, but damn it, she will give him a few scars before it's over. Dandelion wants

to make certain that the son of a bitch has to *earn* her death.

There's the clanking sound of the padlock dropping to the

floor, and she makes a choked blubbering noise in the far back

of her throat. The door swings inward, and shadows dance

around what stands there. The figure allows the bolt cutters to

drop, and he takes a step forward.

This is a different silhouette. Slender, tall, and possessed of

an entirely different aura compared to Uncle. She is having

trouble believing it. Surely she is lost in the ocean of her own

dreams, and this is just something glorious floating in her mind.

Dandelion scrambles over to him, half-limping and half-

crawling, and she uses his pants legs to pull herself up vertically.

She places dainty hands on his chest, the movements nervous

and shaky, hummingbird hands exploring all there is to touch.

Her fingers reach up to hollow cheeks, and they are colder than

a mortuary. She stands on her tippy toes to kiss him, and he braces her lower back to help her reach him. She tastes the tomb. She wraps herself snake-like around a man who thinks that he is dead.

She's ugly-crying now, and he is *real*. He is here. He came for her. His face is pure devotion, and he makes no effort to temper what he feels. Frigid fingertips rise, and he traces the length of her jawline, turning her face up to look at him. He presses an index finger to his lips in a *shh* gesture.

"We have to be quiet. He's asleep in the chair."

"It's you. Here in front of me. It can't be you."

"But it is, Dandelion. I was always meant to be here."

Her throat is working, but the emotion is overwhelming. She can't stop touching him. Caressing what bare skin she can find and tugging at scraps of his clothing. She has imagined this moment in her head a thousand times, but the reality is hard to fathom.

"You're warmer than I expected. Like lava fighting up past a layer of ice."

"That is new, and you are responsible."

He cups her face, and he kisses her deeply. Mummified cinnamon and soil and casket dust. It is the best of all flavors mixed together. His mouth tastes like something undiscovered, a lost archeological find, and she wants to keep exploring that taste until time comes to an end.

A hand with long fingers drifts down and extends to her.

"Come with me. It's time."

She allows her hand to melt into his, and she looks up at him like a submissive prey animal that is being asked to go against its own nature.

"We're really going to do this?"

"Yes."

There is nothing more to be said. Dandelion squeezes his hand as tightly as possible, and Ambrose leads her in the direction of a slumbering devil.

Dandelion

She meekly holds Ambrose's hand and follows along behind him, her head lowered, staring at the floor. Her fingertips explore the veins in his hands, and she focuses on how good they feel. If her eyes stay locked on the veins, she doesn't have to look up at Uncle.

But she hears him. That guttural snoring that comes out of him only when he is lost in the sauce. Dandelion dares to peek, leaning across Ambrose's shoulder and tentatively drinking in the scene. Uncle's big body is welded to the recliner, the torn packaging of a cheap twelve-pack sitting on the floor next to the chair. There are at least seven crumpled aluminum cans littering the area around his feet, so it's clear that he had a little preemptive celebration after locking her in the attic.

Ambrose has an awl in his right hand, and the harsh metal length of it catches the light. His grip on the weapon is tight, and his grip on her is tight too. She's shuffling her feet and struggling to find a secret reserve of courage to draw on, but her nerves are through the roof. Ambrose notices. He pivots and takes her by the chin, pointing to a bare corner of the den.

"Face that wall and close your eyes. Think of the ocean, but not an ocean full of big hungry giants that want to consume you. Picture serenity and calm waters. Float in a salty sea and imagine that you are safe. Can you do that?"

She nods, tears in her eyes, but she doesn't dare let them spill in front of him. She's terrified that the whispering will wake Uncle up.

"I'll call you over when it's time."

Dandelion doesn't argue. She goes over and stands in the corner, and her eyelids flutter closed. She is floating. She is floating. She is *floating*.

Ambrose

Ambrose pictured Uncle as a mythological beast, some great looming presence that would eclipse everyone who ever made the mistake of standing before him. The reality is far more disappointing. Here sits a big, meaty, middle-aged man with booze stains on his tank top and drool on his scruffy chin. But even in his subdued state, there are clues to his brutish nature. Cuts on his knuckles and blood under his fingernails. Ambrose is certain Dandelion is the source of those little wounds.

This man has spent an entire lifetime inflicting wounds on those he deems weaker than himself. Yet here he sleeps like a beer-drunk baby with not a care in the world. Uncle thinks himself untouchable in this house, a holy place where his debauchery has gone unchecked for decades. Ambrose can smell the entitlement that seeps from the old monster's pores, and his newfound rage is renewed.

He does not care if he wakes up. He does not care if it becomes a hardscrabble fight for survival. He intends to bleed this man until he is fully satisfied with the result.

And so that which was once dead steps forward, lifts a glimmering awl, and plunges it into the side of Uncle's torso. He grunts awkwardly, still lost in a soupy drunken fog, and Ambrose stabs him four more times in the side before he even wakes up and realizes what is happening to him. A paw of a hand slaps out, clamping over the new puncture wounds in his side, and Uncle stares up incredulously and tries to figure out what is going on.

Ambrose stabs with mechanical efficiency, the awl rending flesh of chest, arms, and throat. There are little bursts of red spray as arteries are nicked, blood pooling in Uncle's lap, and he has recovered his senses enough to bellow out murky obscenities. His body is feeling overwhelming pressure and heat, and all he sees is a slender shadow that darts right and left, pricking him over and over with some horrifically sharp instrument.

Ambrose makes it a point to target organs next. He snaps the awl forward and punctures liver, pancreas, and Uncle's bowels. There's a foul gassy expulsion as the man's guts get peppered, and he struggles in his own biological stew.

Uncle throws up a forearm and tries to sit up, but Ambrose bends his wrist to the side and buries the awl into a portion of his chest. There's a hideous wheezing noise as the awl pops free from a lung, and Uncle sits there in his bloody clothing and breathes like a drowning rat that has no chance of finding the surface again. It's a tortuous death knell of a sound, and Dandelion covers her ears in the corner and tries not to listen to the wheezing.

"Stop. . .stop. . ."

Uncle looks like a deer that has been shot several times but still hopes for an ounce of mercy. But Ambrose is not in the mood for mercy tonight. He takes up a thin pillow, presses it against Uncle's face, and sends the awl through it numerous times, stabbing his face repeatedly with a growing fervor of passion. Cheek, neck, brow, and even an eyeball are perforated. Words have proven useless for Uncle, so he's mewling now. It is a sad sound to hear coming from a grown man. Ambrose once saw a gore video of a kitten getting its brains squashed out of its ears, and the noise Uncle is making is comparable. The mewling makes him want to hurt Uncle even more, and he pierces him so many times that he loses count. His wrist aches from stabbing, and the pillow tumbles down, blood-speckled feathers drifting up around killer and victim.

Uncle is pissing down his own legs, and his entire shaking body is a waterfall of plasma. He leaks from at least a hundred stab wounds, and still Ambrose finds unmarked sections of flesh to impale.

The man has long given up on fighting back. There was no fight in him to start with due to his inebriated state, but now it is simply an act of slaughter. His bare feet drum the floor and he pales from shock.

Ambrose becomes acutely aware of the smile that has dawned on his own face. He rarely ever shows his teeth in happiness, but it is happening now. His expression is beatific, blood-speckled enamel grinning down at the slab of meat in the chair. It is not so hard to kill a person.

There is passion in this, and of all the fresh emotions that Ambrose has experienced lately, a passion for murder tastes especially sweet on the tongue. No part of him feels dead now. He is here, he is present, and he is stripping the life from this wretched moaning thing. That is power at its apex.

It won't be much longer. Uncle is drowning in his own blood, and several gaping lacerations on his throat are causing him major issues. He is choking and gagging, and bubbles of crimson are popping in his nostrils.

There's this eerie rattling that is developing from his chest, and before it is finished, he wants *her* to see.

"Dandelion."

A hand black with viscera extends to her.

"Come here. Now is the hour of bloodshed."

Dandelion

There are protective dolphins and enchanted rainforest islands that capture her attention, and she is afraid to leave them. She floats without fear, and that is a first. Her mind wants to obsess about what lurks beneath, but she will not allow it. She is in control of her own thoughts. This is her imagination, and the great beaked squids of the deep will remain in the deep where they belong. But she cannot stay. Dandelion is being pulled back to grim reality.

"Now is the hour of bloodshed."

Her eyes finally open, and silent sapphire tears spill down to crisscross her cheeks. She reluctantly turns from the corner and goes to Ambrose. There is a pile of ruined gristle sitting in that chair, vibrating and wheezing like a failing locomotive. Each wheeze expels arterial spray, and Ambrose stands so close that it mists his face with red. Her man seems to savor it.

She holds her body with uncertainty, wrists limp at her sides.

It's not easy to look at what used to be Uncle. She is so accustomed to being abused by him that it puts her into a state of confusion to not have that usual dread spark up in her heart. Still, she hangs back, because even bleeding dogs can find the strength to bite.

But Ambrose is there, hand lowering to brace her lower back and guide her forward. His presence is motivation, and his touch is safety. He places the weight of the awl into her right hand and curls her fingers around it until it feels like an extension of her own limb.

She finally gathers her resolve and looks upon the devil that has lorded over her since childhood. It doesn't even look like a person anymore. It is shaking and pale, borderline pathetic. A sour cut of meat left to drip in the drain of an abattoir.

Ambrose's hand finds the nape of her neck, and he leans over to whisper into her ear.

"Here with you, in this moment, I have never felt more *alive*."

She smiles shyly in spite of the situation. The conviction of his words rings true, because he looks fully alive. Passionate, handsome, and thrumming with pure animal adrenaline. Cotard's delusion has retreated inward, and the apathy seems to have almost leaked from Ambrose, just as all those pints of blood leaked from Uncle.

"But this is your story to finish, Dandelion. He's your kill."

A light touch across the back of her hair for encouragement, and a final whisper before her lover steps back.

"Hold nothing back."

She breathes deeply through her nostrils, filling up her lungs with copper-scented air. Uncle smells like wet pennies, and she's not sure if he recognizes her through the grime of gore that used to be his face. But it doesn't matter. It is a blessing to not be looked at, because his gaze has always been an unwanted intrusion.

She isn't even aware of her own body's motion until it happens. The bobcat shriek that builds up low in her throat and sends saliva splattering out from her lips. The awl floating downward to stab into his groin until she's satisfied with the pop of testicles and the degloving of penile skin. She takes from him those parts that have caused her the most shame and self-loathing.

He is past screaming, so he just trembles, accepting the mutilation. Dandelion lurches to the side and falls against him, pawing at his forehead and pushing the awl down into his ear canal with all the force she can muster. There are brutal squelch noises, and when she yanks out the sharpened point, a faucet of pink flows out. She lifts the awl and studies it, seeing little gray flecks that can only be chunks of punctured brain.

The death rattle increases in intensity, all the mucus and blood and obliterated tissue lodging in Uncle's throat, and finally after what seems like an eon, his perverse spirit departs his physical body. He dies in anguish, filthy and fetid in his own home, and what remains of him slumps down into the chair.

Both Dandelion and Ambrose stand in the ocean of blood that pools outward from the spot of the murder, and they both acknowledge the weight of the moment. It is finished. They have extinguished a human life together.

For this new young couple, it stands as a milestone.

Lovers

Dandelion is wracked with emotion, and she allows the awl

to slip from her fingers and clatter down against the floor.

Ambrose approaches and thrusts his hands into her hair, gently

massaging both roots and scalp. She closes her eyes and leans

back against the comforting weight of his chest.

"You did well."

She turns and looks at him. She takes hold of his hands,

tracing veins, knuckles, and the blackened indentation where a

missing fingernail is finally starting to regrow. Her tongue slips

out to moisten her chapped bottom lip.

"I like your hands."

She lifts his right hand and cups it against her cheek, and her

eyes flash with the implication of lustful violence.

"Use them on me."

Ambrose doesn't hesitate. He slaps her. Hard. The thud of

the impact rocks her head to the side, hair falling into her face,

and she is lost in her own rainbow. The slaps keep coming,

reddening her cheeks with a forced blush, and she is on him

with equal feverish intensity, tearing at his clothes and ripping

the shirt from his thin body. They slip against the blood on the

floorboards, and they fall in each other's arms, cradling and

suckling and tangling together like starved insects.

Ambrose is choking her, and Dandelion sees nothing but

pleasant stars. Her clothes have practically evaporated, naked

and vulnerable now, and she tugs his jeans off and throws them

over the corpse of Uncle. There are tender burn scars on the

shaft of his cock, and the sight of them makes her smile.

She sees so many parts of his body that she likes, and so she

decides to bite them all. She gnaws on his flesh, leaving deep

purple marks, and her tongue lashes from her mouth to heat up

his coldness. He cranks her neck to the side and when he finally enters her, it is like being impaled by a ragged icicle. It feels fucking *divine*, and the mere act changes her. They fuck and cry and scream and roar together. Both of their nude bodies are slick with blood, soaked in crimson, and Dandelion creates artistic handprints on Ambrose's pallid skin. Their eye contact never stops, and in each other, they find a perfect swirling limbo.

She opens her mouth wide and her man spits in it, baptizing her in saliva and the plasma of a fallen tormentor. It tastes good. The delicious flavor of *soulmate*.

It goes on and on until they're both exhausted, bruised, bitten, and wholeheartedly violated. They become a beast with two scarlet-drenched backs, and there is no telling where Dandelion ends and Ambrose begins.

Lovers sore and sullied, the cadaver in the recliner momentarily forgotten. There is only this ruined, interlocked bliss, and both of them are terrified to let it fade.

Aftermath

They languish together in the clawfoot bathtub, listening to the wind play at the neglected rooftop of the Victorian. Dandelion leans back against Ambrose, hair lank and multi-colored around her shoulders. There are haunted circles beneath her eyes, and the eyes themselves are strangely vacant. Both their bodies ache from what feels like a thousand carnal insults. Steam enshrouds them, and the tepid water of the bath is stained carmine from all the blood.

"The body. What happens now?"

"I've researched dissolving a corpse in a barrel of acid. They become just boiling soup after awhile. Soon I'll go to the hardware store and get what we need to make that happen."

Dandelion inhales deeply and allows herself to sink a few inches further into the water. She wants to feel free, but a part of her feels somehow lost. Wandering unfamiliar plateaus with no fixed destination.

"Do you think we'll last, Ambrose? Now that we're finally together with no obstacle between us."

Ambrose leans his head back and rests his skull on porcelain. His hair is twisted up into a crown of horns from the water. His fingertips keep playing across the fragility of her collarbones.

"In another life. In another place. In another universe. It doesn't matter, Dandelion."

He cranes his neck closer, and his bruised lips find her ear.

"I think that we are destined to hurt each other forever."

There is stillness after that. Unspoken promises of pain. A lifetime of lament. The dark in her settling companionably against the dark in him. She pictures a wooded path that carries the assurance of balanced violence. Their impulses and desires and private brutalities eroding one another until neither are recognizable as what they once were.

Steam, wind, and blood swirling down the drain.

Dandelion ducks her head under the water, holds her breath,

and wonders when the monsters will find her again.

About The Author

Jeremy Megargee has always loved dark fiction. He cut his teeth on R.L Stine's Goosebumps series as a child and a fascination with Stephen King, Jack London, Algernon Blackwood, and many others followed later in life. Jeremy weaves his tales of personal horror from Martinsburg, West Virginia with his cat Lazarus acting as his muse/familiar. He is a native of Appalachia and you can often find him peddling his dark words in various mountain hollers deep within the wilderness.

CROWN OF CARRION

A werewolf novella from Jeremy Megargee

There's a homestead deep in the mountains called Merkel Valley and werewolves den there. They're a peaceful clan, focused on hunting game animals and preserving the traditions of Mother Moon from one generation to the next.

But there's unrest in the pack, and it comes in the form of a rogue wolf named Merrill Sade. Banished long ago from Merkel Valley, Merrill has made his mark in the cities below with tooth and claw. He is a zealot obsessed with stories about an old feral god lost to time, and now commands a ragtag band of cannibals that serve at his heel. Merrill's thoughts are rabid, and he has no qualms about wetting his fangs
with innocent blood.

He seeks the remnants of a powerful relic known as the Crown of Carrion. If found, they open a doorway to a ravenous force that howls across space and time. All that stands against him is his former lover Ivy, and a few brave wolves from Merkel Valley who are willing to take a stand against Merrill's unrepentant bloodshed.

Will peace prevail in Merkel Valley, or will Merrill and his cannibals feast on this world until nothing is left
but gristle and dust?